D0108351

Marrying
MALCOLM
MURGATROYD

MAME FARRELL

A Sunburst Book
Farrar · Straus · Giroux

The Library of Congress has cataloged the hardcover edition as follows:
Farrell, Mame.
    Marrying Malcolm Murgatroyd / Mame Farrell.— 1st ed.
        p.   cm.
    Summary: Hannah Billings hates being teased about marrying
Malcolm Murgatroyd, the most unpopular and misunderstood boy
in her sixth-grade class, until he reveals his true personality when
her brother succumbs to muscular dystrophy.
    ISBN-13: 978-0-374-44744-1 (pbk.)
    ISBN-10: 0-374-44744-6 (pbk.)
    [1. Interpersonal relations—Fiction.   2. Popularity—Fiction.
3. Muscular dystrophy—Fiction.   4. Physically handicapped—Fiction.]
I. Title.
PZ7.F2455Mar   1995
[Fic]—dc20   95-5420

With all my love to Shannon and Ricky,
who give me everything . . . Even time

Marrying
MALCOLM
MURGATROYD

one

THE FIRST TIME Malcolm Murgatroyd actually connected with a kickball, he got so excited he ran the bases backward. It was pitiful—poor Malcolm, forgetting at first to run at all, and then going off in that stupid gallop of his to third base, then second, then first. He didn't even know he'd done anything wrong. It was terrible. This was three years ago, when we were in third grade.

The kids on our team were yelling and throwing their hands up and shouting, "Malcolm, you jerk! You're going the wrong way!" The kids on Mrs. Birmingham's team were cracking up and screaming, "Way to go, Malcolm! Way to go!"

Like I said, it was terrible.

The kids on Mrs. Birmingham's team said it was a reverse run; Eddie Baker called it an "un-run" and said our team had to give up one of the runs we'd already scored. Bruce Wyatt threw a fit, since he had scored all three of our runs—as usual—and Dennis Duffy kicked so much dirt on home plate that Mrs. Birmingham threw him out of the game.

Our substitute, Miss Spalding, just stood there; she was responsible for Malcolm getting into the game. She was only a sub and didn't know the "rules." Malcolm never played kickball or dodgeball or anything with us. We wouldn't let him. Our regular teacher, Mrs. Hinton, had quit trying to get Malcolm picked for a team months ago. But Miss Spalding, being young and not used to third graders, insisted we let him have his ups. And he did.

I thought Bruce was going to clobber Malcolm on the spot. "Murgadork! You imbecile!"

Malcolm was smiling. He was bouncing on the balls of his feet. I suppose he still thought he'd done something good.

"Quit bouncing!" Bruce's face was almost purple. "Stand still, you creep, so I can bash you!"

I guess that was when Malcolm realized his mistake. But he didn't apologize. All he said was "I'm telling!"

That was one of Malcolm's biggest problems. He told. He told on everybody. He'd even tell on Bruce Wyatt, which was the stupidest thing anybody could do. You just didn't tell on Bruce Wyatt.

"Baby!"

Malcolm scrunched his nose up. "Telling!"

"Sissy! Baby! Sissy-baby-creepo jerk!"

"Telling, telling, telling, *telling*!"

Bruce's fists were clenched. He walked right up to Malcolm (who was half Bruce's size) and bent down to look at him. Their noses were almost touching. "Oh yeah?"

Then Malcolm was calling, "Miss Spaaalllllding!"

But before the substitute could arrive on the scene, I snuck up behind Bruce and said, "Just leave him alone."

Bruce whirled. When he saw it was me, his purple cheeks began to soften until they were a bright, embarrassed pink. "But, Hannah . . ." He kicked at a stone on the ground.

"Please. Leave him alone, okay? Please?"

"Okay. But he's benched! He's not allowed to play anymore! Not on my team."

Malcolm opened his mouth to protest, but I stopped him

with a look. Another of Malcolm's problems was he didn't know to quit while he was ahead—or while he still had a head. His jaw snapped shut and he turned and slunk off toward the jungle gym.

"Can I walk you home after school, Hannah?" Bruce was asking.

My eyes were still on Malcolm and I sighed at what I noticed. "Sure, Bruce," I said, but inside I was hoping that the nurse had a dry pair of underpants in Malcolm's size.

"Miss Spalding?"

"Yes?"

"Malcolm Murgatroyd peed on himself."

She looked at me, horrified. "He what?"

You heard me, I thought. But I repeated, "He peed. In his pants. He had an accident."

"Oh my!" She looked like she might cry.

"I'll take him to the nurse," I told her. In third grade, taking Malcolm Murgatroyd to the nurse was my job. "She usually keeps extra underwear in her office for emergencies," I explained.

Miss Spalding was chewing her nails. The trouble with the nurse's underwear stash was it was mostly kindergartener-sized, since generally it was the little kids who had accidents. You'd think after all this time the nurse would keep a special pair just for Malcolm—after all, he was one of her best customers.

That was third grade.

In fourth grade, one of Malcolm's big problems was sneakers. He was always about a year behind in sneakers. In other words, in fourth grade, he wore the sneakers that were cool in third grade; in fifth grade, he had the sneakers he should have had in fourth.

I happened to know this was not entirely Malcolm's fault.

His mother liked to buy things on sale (even though Malcolm's dad is a very successful surgeon and they have plenty of money) and one of the first things to get marked down for the back-to-school sales in September is last year's sneakers. So Malcolm always started school in a kind of sneaker time warp.

In fifth grade, Malcolm got his braces off. His teeth, like his brain, must have been way ahead of his body—his baby teeth fell out and his crooked, jumbled-up, permanent ones came in long before anyone else's. So he was ready for braces when a lot of us were still counting our change from the tooth fairy and whistling through the gaps in our gums. Malcolm's braces went on early and they came off early; he was finishing up with his orthodontia just as most of the kids in our grade were starting with theirs. I had hoped this would work in Malcolm's favor, since getting rid of braces is usually a big plus, dentally *and* socially speaking. But for some reason it worked against Malcolm. His teeth seemed uncommonly large, since we were so used to seeing them all fenced in behind wire and metal. He looked like a Shetland pony to us. Then, for the first month or so after the braces came off, Malcolm would click his tongue against his bare teeth. It drove us nuts. He was just so weird! And the worst part was that he seemed to enjoy being weird. He was also very, very smart, which wasn't exactly his fault, either. His mom was as big on getting good grades as she was on getting bargains.

I know all this because Dr. and Mrs. Murgatroyd are my parents' best friends in the whole world. As my dad likes to say, they go "way back," so consequently Malcolm and I go way back, too, like since birth, and it's been a mystery to me how a mom and dad as cool as the Murgatroyds could wind up with such a nerd for a kid.

The thing was, I didn't know that Malcolm was a loser until we wound up in the same second-grade class.

On the first day of second grade, everything changed. One minute we were a bunch of little kids who'd been going to school together since kindergarten, and the next, we were hanging around in clusters on the playground. There was the studious cluster, the shy cluster, the cluster with the best clothes—and there was that one, really important cluster. It was so important that it wasn't just a cluster; it was an out-and-out clique. It was the Popular Kids.

I still don't know why I wound up with the Popular Kids. It wasn't that I thought I belonged there. Maybe it was because Bruce Wyatt had smiled at me and said, "Hannah. Over here."

And there I was. Unfortunately, the first order of business seemed to be pointing out the kids who had no hope of ever becoming one of us. Malcolm, it turned out, was the unanimous favorite. That was the day I made him promise never to tell the kids about our families' being best friends. Of course no one in the clique, not even Bruce, came right out and told me I couldn't be friends with Malcolm. I figured that out for myself. And the surprising thing was that Malcolm didn't even question me on it. I asked. He agreed. It was that simple.

Malcolm never found a cluster. The studious kids had seemed to be his best bet, but even back then, he had a tendency to brag about how smart he was. I guess even studious kids get tired of hearing about how studious other people are. So Malcolm was clusterless.

"Malcolm will surprise you one of these days!" my mother always said. "You wait and see, Hannah." She'd grin at me and say, "Then you'll be proud to marry him!"

"Mother!"

"You wait and see," she'd say and smile. "Malcolm Murgatroyd is going to be a late bloomer."

But who wants to marry a late bloomer?

two

My mother and my little brother, Ian, were helping me sort through old photographs for my first sixth-grade project. The assignment was to write my autobiography, and I'd get extra credit for including pictures. Mom thought it would be a great opportunity to organize all the snapshots we had lying around the house, and in boxes in the attic. The problem was most of them were of us doing stuff with the Murgatroyds. The snapshots were scattered all over the floor and the coffee table; a bunch were piled in Ian's lap.

"You sure had a wacky haircut in this one!" Ian said to me.

I leaned up over the wheel of his chair to see. He was holding my second-grade class picture, the one of all the kids sitting in rows. "Ugh! Looks like I have a dead rabbit stuck on my head."

My mother laughed. "There's a lovely thought!"

"Look at Malcolm," said Ian.

I looked. I remembered. Malcolm was holding his lunch box between his knees. Second grade was the Year of the Lunch Box.

"Whoever heard of holding a lunch box in a class picture?" Ian asked, not unkindly.

Second grade was the year Malcolm refused to let go of his lunch box, ever. He cried for fifteen minutes before the teacher and the photographer agreed to let him hold it in the picture. I sighed, studying the photo. It was a stupid lunch box covered with pictures of tropical fish.

"Here's one," said Mom, "from our first summer at the shore." She handed me a snapshot. I was about four, sitting on my father's shoulders. You could hardly recognize Malcolm. He had on a big hooded sweatshirt and a towel around his bottom half, because he sunburned so easily; there were gobs of white gunk on his nose and lips. Dr. Murgatroyd was spinning a volleyball on his index finger. He was what my father called "a real jock."

"Where was I?" Ian wanted to know.

Mom patted her tummy. "About three weeks away!" She handed us another picture across the coffee table. "See?"

"Wow! You were huge!"

Ian craned his neck to see. "Fatso!"

"Well," said Mom, "eight months of pregnancy will do that to you!"

The picture was of my mother and Mrs. Murgatroyd on the deck of the Murgatroyds' beach house. The twins, Celeste and Olivia, were clinging to Mrs. Murgatroyd's ankles. She was wearing a bikini and looked glamorous. My mom looked liked she was wearing an inner tube *under* her swimsuit.

Ian took the picture from me. "You look so happy," he murmured sadly, and I knew exactly what he meant.

So did Mom. She slid down from the couch and knelt beside him. "Ian, honey . . ."

I looked away. There were tears in my brother's voice. "You were happy 'cause you didn't know I was going to have muscular dystrophy. You thought I'd be perfect."

"C'mon, Ian," I began, but my voice broke.

"You're better than perfect," said Mom gently.

Now Ian's eyes went back to the picture of my second-grade class; he focused on Malcolm. Then there was the electrical whir of his wheelchair as he left the living room. In a moment, we heard him on the telephone.

"Hello, Kate, is Malcolm home?"

Mom stood up and smoothed my hair. "He'll talk to Malcolm. He'll feel better."

I nodded. If anybody could cheer Ian up, Malcolm could.

My best friend, Evie Neville, was coming for dinner and sleeping over. Dad was barbecuing on the patio. Evie loves barbecue. The doorbell rang just as Dad was lighting the grill.

"That kid has charcoal radar!" Dad teased.

I skipped through the house and answered the door.

"Hey, Billings!"

"Hey, Neville!"

Evie stepped in. In the distance, I heard Ian's chair clunking into a piece of furniture.

"How's he doing in that thing?" Evie asked softly. She looked nervous.

"He's getting used to it. He's not so great at U-turns, but he does all right on the straightaway."

Evie looked at the ground.

"Anyway"—I lowered my voice to a whisper—"did you bring it?"

She nodded, smiling. "Tons!"

After dinner, we were going to experiment with Evie's sister's blush, lipstick, eyeliner, and mascara. I couldn't wait.

Mom was fitting the last of the snapshots into an album when we passed through the living room.

"Hi, Evie."

"Hi, Mrs. Billings. Whatcha doin'?"

"Just organizing some memories."

"Pictures?" Evie beamed. "Can I see?"

My heart stopped. Mom was about to hand over the photo album. I practically shouted "No!" and they both looked at me, surprised. "You don't want to see those stupid pictures," I said quickly. "They're boring, even to me, and I'm in most of them."

"I want to see what you looked like before I met you," said Evie, who'd moved to town only a year ago.

"I looked like I had a dead rabbit stuck on my head," I told her.

"What?"

My mother was frowning. I think she knew what was up.

"C'mon," I said to Evie, eager to escape Mom's look. "Let's go upstairs." I winked at her, which meant: I want to check out the makeup before dinner. She got it.

"Oh, okay."

In my room she dumped the contents of her bag on my bed. She hadn't been kidding when she'd said tons.

We sorted through it. She had Luscious Peach lipstick, Silk Smoke eye shadow, and Mysterious Midnight mascara. Moonshadow Mauve was the color of the eyeliner, whatever Moonshadow Mauve was.

"Looks purple to me," I said.

"Hannah!" came my mother's voice up the stairs. Evie threw herself across the pile of cosmetics on the bed. "Come set the table!"

"Stay here," I told Evie. "Hide it." That was fine with Evie. She hates setting the table.

Mom gave me an icy look when I found her in the kitchen. Through the big window in the breakfast nook, I could see that the patio table was already set.

"Tell me why you wouldn't let Evie look at the pictures."

I shrugged.

"Hannah . . ."

"You know why, Mom! Because."

"Because of Malcolm?"

I stared past her, focusing on the umbrella shading the patio table. "I guess."

Mom let out a deep sigh. "That's awful, Hannah."

"I know." And I did know. But what was I supposed to do? "Nobody at school knows, Mom. Well, I mean, they know Malcolm is friends with Ian and all, but they'd never let me hear the end of it if they knew my whole family actually hangs around with Malcolm's whole family! They'd laugh me right out of sixth grade!" And they would, too.

"We do more than just 'hang around,' " said Dad, appearing from outside. He looked as ticked-off as Mom. "The Murgatroyds are our best friends. I'm Olivia's godfather, for Pete's sake."

I wanted to say, Big Whoop for you. Instead, I said, "I know. Dr. Steve and Kate are cool. But Malcolm . . . isn't."

Mom went to the refrigerator and removed a platter of steaks. "I suppose 'cool' is the only thing that matters?"

I tugged at my long ponytail. "I just don't want my friends to think I'm a geek." There! I'd admitted it. What more did they want?

"If they'd think that, then they aren't very good friends, are they?"

I knew she was going to say that. It was such a mom-ish thing to say. I rolled my eyes.

My father was searching in a drawer for the barbecue tongs. "The kids know Ian likes Malcolm. Do they think he's a geek?"

I shifted my weight and studied the floor tiles. "I don't know what they think about Ian," I said, pointedly. "Nobody'll talk to me about him." Secretly, I was scared to even guess what my friends thought about Ian and Malcolm's friendship. The word "misfits" came to mind. I shook the thought out of my head and looked up at my father. "Besides, it's different with Ian." Talk about your understatements.

Then we heard Evie bounding down the stairs and the subject was closed. Or so I thought. Evie took the ice bucket and followed my dad out to the patio. I was about to join them with the lemonade, but Mom stopped me.

"Ian asked if he could invite Malcolm over tonight," she said quietly.

I froze. My face must have gone perfectly white. "Mom, no! He can't."

"Oh, Hannah." She planted her hands on her hips and looked very annoyed.

"Tell Ian that Malcolm can't come. Please." The panic was like a small explosion in my stomach. Evie, like the other kids at school, knew Ian and Malcolm were friends. But having her and Malcolm at the dinner table together scared me. I was reasonably sure that Malcolm would hold up his end of our pact, but my parents and Ian were another story. They could easily say something like "Remember the time we all went skiing in Colorado, Malcolm?" or "Hannah, you and Malcolm were so cute when you danced together at the Murgatroyds' anniversary party." Those topics didn't come up often, but it was still too big a risk.

"Evie is your best friend. Do you really think she'd care?"

I didn't want to chance it. "Please, Mom!"

"I can't believe how selfish you're being. Your brother wants to invite a friend—"

I cut her off, fuming. "You give in to him all the time, just because he's in that stupid wheelchair." As soon as I said it, I wished I could swallow the words up. It was the worst thing I'd ever said in my life.

Mom's eyes flashed. From the way she snatched up the

bottle of steak sauce, I could tell she wasn't happy with me at all. But she nodded, and said softly and slowly, "Okay, Hannah. But I want you to know I'm disappointed in you." She turned and marched out to the patio.

Fine. Be disappointed, I thought. But I felt miserable. I'd gotten my way, but I felt crummy. I felt like the crummiest person in the world. I made my way out to the patio, but my appetite was gone. Even for barbecue.

three

MY FATHER AND DR. MURGATROYD were almost finished
with Ian's new bedroom. Dad, who's an architect, had de-
signed an addition on the first floor with an extra-wide doorway and low light switches that Ian could reach. There was
even a special-sized bathroom just for him. Now I'd have my
own bathroom upstairs, the one we used to share.

Mom and I had painted the upstairs bathroom pale yellow
and bought a pretty floral shower curtain at Laura Ashley.
With my birthday money I got some yellow-and-white guest
towels, which I arranged perfectly on the towel rack. My
bubble bath and powder looked just right on the vanity. Evie
had left me a lipstick; I put some on and hid it under the
washcloths in a drawer. Then I dumped all of Ian's old bath
toys and dinosaur soaps into a laundry basket and carried them
downstairs.

I found him in the doorway of the addition. It smelled like
new wood and sawdust and carpet glue. Dad and Dr. Steve
were around the corner in Ian's bathroom, grouting the tile.

"It looks great," I observed, leaning around the wheelchair.

"Yeah. Look." He rolled in and flipped on the lights with
a switch that was about even with my waist. "I can reach."

I placed the laundry basket in the center of the room and

sat on his bed. "Think you'll like living down here?" I asked.

"It'll be better than being carried upstairs every night," he replied, shrugging. I nodded. The muscular dystrophy had gotten bad only three months ago; it was still very new to him. To all of us.

"I like the carpet. Neat color."

"Will you help me unpack my books?"

"Sure." Three big boxes were piled in the corner. For a third-grader, Ian was an excellent reader. That was one of the things he and Malcolm had in common. "Do they go in any special order?" I asked, opening the top carton.

Ian rolled his eyes. "Alphabetical, doy-brain. But keep all the science-fiction stuff together. Wait—" He wheeled himself over to the boxes. The chair left two thin furrows in the new carpet. "Let me do the sci-fi. I've got a system. Ackcherly, it's Malcolm's system."

I knelt down beside the long row of built-in shelves Dad had made. That was when Malcolm appeared in the doorway, clicking his tongue against his teeth.

"Howdy, alien."

Ian's face lit up. "Greetings, Earth being!"

That was their new game. The day Ian got the electric wheelchair, which did sort of look like a spaceship, Malcolm came up with the alien-Earthling act. Ian had been feeling pretty strange about it until Malcolm thought up the game. As usual, Malcolm—the biggest geek in the sixth grade— knew exactly what to do to make Ian feel better.

"Howdy, Hannah."

I shoved *The Wind in the Willows* into the shelf. "Hi."

While Malcolm and Ian were exchanging their Top Secret Intergalactic Handshake, I looked long and hard at Malcolm, trying to figure out what it was that made him such a drip. His shirt wasn't buttoned all the way up to the collar, and his jeans weren't a mile too short, which was always the case with nerds on TV. I decided that Malcolm's problem couldn't be solved by just unbuttoning a button, or letting down a hem. It wasn't just something on the outside, like clothes. It was his overall Malcolmness that did it to him. And as far as I could tell, he was stuck with it. I sighed, and decided that the people who write TV shows with nerd characters would do well to spend a little time with Malcolm. Go right to the source. Because Malcolm was the genuine article.

"What's that on your lips?" Malcolm asked me.

"It's lipstick, you dipstick."

Ian laughed.

"It's a strange color!" Malcolm observed.

He was really burning me up. "It's called Luscious Peach, and for your information it's a very expensive color that you can only get at Lord and Taylor. It was Evie's but she gave it to me."

"Lipstick for Bruce Wyatt?" Malcolm sneered.

I slammed *Charlie and the Chocolate Factory* onto the shelf. "What's it to you, Malcolm?"

Ian wheeled over to Malcolm. Now there was a tic-tac-toe board of wheel ruts in the carpet. "Does Hannah like Bruce Wyatt?"

Malcolm nodded. "All the girls like Bruce Wyatt. But he likes Hannah!"

"But aren't *you* going to marry Hannah?" Ian sounded very concerned. I felt my stomach turn.

Dad came out of the bathroom, chuckling. "That's the plan!" He had sticky white goop all over his jeans.

Boy, I hated this conversation. But I was also used to it. They'd decided to marry me off to Malcolm when I was about two months old! If Malcolm had been half as cute as his father, Dr. Steve, I wouldn't have minded one bit.

Dr. Steve popped out from Ian's bathroom, singing "Here comes the bride."

Malcolm was blushing, as he always did when this god-awful topic came up. And, as always, I felt sick.

Dr. Steve said, "What's the matter, Hannah? Cold feet?"

I got up to leave and almost tripped over Ian's Hardy Boys collection.

"The Earth Princess is escaping!" Ian cried. "Secure all exits."

Too late. I was upstairs in my yellow bathroom, smearing off the lipstick. From now on, Luscious Peach was reserved for Bruce Wyatt only.

We found out Ian had muscular dystrophy when he was five and a half. I was almost eight and scared to death. *Muscular dystrophy*—it sounded painful, incredibly painful. It sounded like forever.

Pneumonia. That was the other ugly word I heard them say, the word that made my mother cry.

That afternoon, Malcolm and I sat on the low wall of the Murgatroyds' back patio and watched Ian play in the sandbox. The grownups were inside, talking. Dr. Steve was bringing my mom an aspirin.

Malcolm looked at Ian. "It will be up to us," he told me. "Most of it, anyway."

I wasn't sure what he meant. He was already eight and about a million times smarter than me. "What will be up to us?" I asked.

Malcolm shrugged. "Making sure he doesn't give up. After all, when he can't walk anymore . . ."

I felt as if I'd been socked in the stomach, like I'd had the wind knocked out of me. "What do you mean, 'when he can't walk'?" Nobody'd said anything about that.

"That's what happens."

"Well . . ." I felt like I'd lost all the words I'd ever known. "When?"

He shrugged again.

"They didn't tell me," I whispered. We were silent, watching Ian fill a pail with sand and dump it out, again and again. "He looks so . . . regular. He looks okay."

"It's going to be up to us."

I nodded. But, as it turned out, most of it was up to Malcolm.

four

BEFORE SCHOOL, I MET EVIE in the girls' lav and we put some makeup on. I'd brought along the Luscious Peach; she had blush and something called concealer, which she said was for zits and dark circles.

"Dark circles?"

"Under your eyes. Like from not enough sleep." Neither of us had zits and we'd both gotten plenty of sleep, so we stuck to the blush and the lipstick.

"Well?"

I looked at her. "You've got some lipstick on your teeth."

Sheila McElroy came in. "Makeup! Where'd ya get it!"

Evie took on her sophisticated tone. "My sister gave it to me."

"Cool!" Sheila seemed envious, but didn't ask to use any of the stuff. I was glad. I didn't mind sharing stuff with Evie, my best friend, but who wanted Sheila McElroy's cooties?

"Bruce Wyatt has the coolest jeans on today," said Sheila, and gave me a look. "I sat with him on the bus."

Sheila knew I liked Bruce, and she probably knew Bruce liked me, but she was not the type to let that bother her.

I tried to look busy with the Luscious Peach and she changed the subject.

"Guess who they just made hall monitor! El Nerdo himself. Malcolm Murgatroyd."

Evie snapped her compact shut. "Figures."

"He's acting like he's the boss of everybody. He thinks he's Mr. Great now, just because he's monitor." Sheila was brushing her wavy red hair.

"Monitor is so dumb!" said Evie.

I didn't say anything.

Monitor wasn't dumb. In fact, it was sort of an honor. It meant the teachers thought you had leadership qualities and all that junk. I knew Malcolm; he was probably very proud of himself. And I wondered, if Bruce Wyatt or Dennis Duffy had gotten hall monitor, would Evie and Sheila have called it dumb. I doubted it.

Then I did say something. I said, "Yeah. Monitor is so dumb." I didn't bother to mention that I was *engaged* to the hall monitor.

"I don't think Malcolm ever washes his hair," Sheila said, opening the lavatory door. "It's so ishy and oily."

"What's ishy mean?" I asked, although I had a pretty good idea.

Sheila wrinkled her nose. "Something is ishy that makes you go, 'Ish.' "

That was a typical Sheila answer, but I didn't feel like challenging her. She'd made her point—Malcolm's hair had an oil problem. Next time I saw Mrs. Murgatroyd I'd mention that. Somehow.

Evie and I split up outside the sixth-grade classrooms. She had Mrs. Blake, I had Miss Lindstrum. "See you at lunch," I said.

"See ya."

In one corner of my class, the boys were looking at some sports magazine. Bruce Wyatt was one of them. I wished I had an excuse to talk to him so he'd notice the lipstick before it wore off. Malcolm was sitting by himself. His hall monitor's badge caught the autumn sun and reflected it up into his eyeglasses, making them look blank. Like he had no eyeballs.

Any other kid who'd been appointed hall monitor would have taken that stupid badge off the minute his or her morning patrol was over with. Not Malcolm. I was sure he intended to wear that thing for the rest of the day. Maybe the rest of his life, unless they made him give it back when school let out in June. So there he was, wearing his badge during morning announcements, the Pledge of Allegiance, lunch count, and Miss Lindstrum's vocabulary lesson. To him, the badge said, "I am important. I am in charge."

To us that badge spelled NERD.

Bruce Wyatt was slipping me a note. I pretended to drop my pencil and snatched the note out of his hand. I felt a little tingle in my spine when his fingers brushed against my wrist.

"We're switching lunches on Murgatroyd. Want to help?"

I sank slightly in my chair. It was so stupid when they did that. Switching lunches meant each kid would take a turn sneaking into the coatroom and lifting the good stuff out of Malcolm's lunch bag and replacing it with something skuzzy.

The skuzzy stuff was usually gobs of paste and pencil shavings mixed together and smeared on bread from a sandwich someone was willing to give up from his own lunch. Once, Dennis found a dead toad on his way to school and put that in Malcolm's bag. I really despised the lunch switching. I hated thinking of Kate standing over the kitchen counter, mixing perfectly good tuna salad for Malcolm's lunch, her long, perfect fingernails clicking against the mayonnaise jar. Then carefully cutting and peeling an apple and wrapping it in foil. Then the napkin, the juice box . . . And then there was Malcolm, sitting alone in the lunchroom with nothing to eat.

"I don't think you should switch his lunch," I wrote back. "I heard Miss Lindstrum tell Mrs. Blake that the next time Malcolm's lunch got messed with, she was giving the whole class detention." Of course, I hadn't heard any such thing. It was a bluff—hopefully, a good one. Then I wrote: "P.S. Nice jeans."

I folded the note and dropped it over my shoulder on Bruce's desk.

It took him a while to write back. He must have been thinking about it.

"Thanks for the warning," he wrote, finally. "I guess we better not." I sighed, relieved, and kept reading. "We'll do something to him in art."

I couldn't imagine anything that could be done to Malcolm in art being as bad as finding paste and reptiles in his lunch bag, so I relaxed. A little.

Miss Lindstrum was adjusting the blinds to keep the sun from blinking off Malcolm's badge. Then I noticed something sticking out of Malcolm's desk: Cecil. Cecil the stuffed seal.

The sixth-grade hall monitor had brought a stuffed animal to school.

It was going to be a long day.

five

THEY STOLE CECIL, that's what they did in art.

Not that Malcolm didn't sort of have it coming to him. I mean, in sixth grade you just don't bring your teddy bear or whatever to school. Cecil got the worst of it, actually. Cecil got it in art.

Malcolm had acquired Cecil the summer he and I were four years old and our families were together in Ocean City. On the boardwalk, my dad won me a big green pig (stuffed, of course), and Dr. Steve won Cecil for Malcolm. That night, we both slept with our new animals, but we were four then and it was okay. I happened to know (Ian told me) that Malcolm still slept with Cecil. In spite of that, after all these years, Cecil was in pretty good shape—until Dennis got hold of him. Dennis threw Cecil across the room to Bruce.

"Give him back," moaned Malcolm in his whiniest voice, "or I'm telling!"

"Clam up, Murgaturd!" Bruce ordered, catching the seal midflight with a leaning grab. The art teacher, Mr. Finch, had left the room to refill his coffee mug.

I kept my head down and worked furiously on my macaroni mosaic project. In my opinion, we'd outgrown pasta art back in the third grade, but Mr. Finch wasn't much of an art teacher. At the moment, I was just happy to be involved in any assignment that would keep my eyes off the hullabaloo being caused by Cecil. I kept my head down, furiously gluing small macaroni shells in a row beside a circle of elbows. Give it back, I willed silently. C'mon, Bruce, just give it back.

The next thing I knew, Cecil was missing both eyes and most of his left front foot. Or should I say fin?

"Bruce," I said. "Cut it out." Malcolm's badge was flashing like crazy, bouncing light toward the ceiling and off the fourth grade's aluminum-foil mobiles hanging there. He was crying, as if his own left fin—or foot—had been torn off. "Give him back the seal, Bruce! Dennis!"

But Cecil was now striped with purple-and-orange paint and had ziti glued to most of his fur.

"Take your sissy seal!" cried Dennis, laughing. Bruce tossed Cecil in a long, high arc across the room, purple-and-orange paint spattering as he flew.

Too late, the art teacher returned. Malcolm was whimpering and pulling the stuck macaroni (along with big tufts of seal fluff) off Cecil's once-silver body. "Mr. Finch . . . they killed Cecil!"

At the news of a murder, Mr. Finch seemed pretty shaken up. He scanned the room as though he thought Cecil was a student.

Malcolm marched up to Mr. Finch, cradling the stuffed animal in his arms. "See?"

I noticed Bruce and Dennis were suddenly very involved with their mosaics. Dennis had a whole box of spaghetti dumped out in front of him.

"It's only watercolor paint," I said, standing and making my way toward Malcolm and the teacher.

Bruce looked up quickly, then back down at his project. I

heard him whisper to McElroy, "Why does Hannah always stick up for that nerd?"

"Because Hannah is a *nice person*," Sheila said, but it didn't sound like a compliment.

"We can rinse him in the janitor's sink," I said to Mr. Finch.

"That's kind of you, Miss Billings," said the teacher, who then took a big swallow of his coffee. I hoped it was boiling hot and burned his tongue; if he hadn't gone out to fill his coffee mug, none of this would have happened. And then I wouldn't have had to explain to the other kids why—again —I flew to Malcolm's rescue.

I was running out of lies.

The janitor's closet with the big dirty sink in it was downstairs. I kept a good five feet in front of Malcolm the whole way, in case anyone was roaming the halls. The last thing I wanted was to be seen alone with Malcolm, especially when he was carrying that beat-up stuffed animal around.

And crying.

"Quit crying, Malcolm. We'll clean him up."

Malcolm sniffed and pulled the remains of Cecil's front fin out of a pocket. "What about this?" he snuffled, swinging the missing limb in front of my face.

"Your mom can sew it on. It's not that big a deal."

The janitor's closet smelled of dust and floor wax. I pulled the string to light the bare bulb overhead, then ran the cold and hot water until the flow was lukewarm.

"Give it."

Malcolm handed over the ruined seal. "Careful."

Most of the paint came off, but Cecil was barely recognizable when I was done. So much of his fur was missing where Malcolm had pulled the macaroni off that the seal looked as if he had mange. He was finless on one side, and his plastic eyes were gone.

"Kate can use buttons for eyes," I assured Malcolm, who was holding the soggy little beast tenderly.

"Thanks, Hannah."

"No problem. Just don't . . ."

"I know, I know. Don't tell anybody about our—relationship."

I winced. "Don't call it that." I thought I noticed a hint of a smile on his face when he said "relationship."

I decided to try to clue him in, as long as we were secluded in the privacy of the janitor's closet. "Listen, Malcolm. I'm getting a little fed up with bailing you out all the time. And the kids are starting to get suspicious about it." I sat on an upside-down bucket. "My reputation for being a nice person can only take me so far, ya know? I mean, I've been like your guardian angel or something since second grade . . . Nobody's *that* nice. Sooner or later, the kids are gonna realize I've got"—I tried to remember a phrase from the mystery movie Evie and I had seen on television—"ulterior motives. They're gonna figure out about our families and stuff."

Malcolm wrung out Cecil's tail into the sink. Over the tinkling of the water he said, "So what do you want me to do about it?"

"Stop screwing up! Stop doing stupid things like wearing your badge all day and bringing stuffed animals to school." I sighed. "You should have known they'd pick on you for that, Malcolm."

"Maybe I didn't care."

"Well, I care."

His face brightened, and I added quickly, "I care about having to come to your rescue every time you do something stupid, that's what I care about. You could make it a lot easier for me if you'd just try to fit in a little."

"Fitting in's not so great." He shook Cecil out a bit; purplish and orangish drops of water splattered his glasses.

I narrowed my eyes. "How would you know?"

He shrugged. "Because you fit in, and you look pretty miserable to me."

I shot up off the bucket. "Because you make me miserable, Malcolm!"

He turned his nose up. For a nerd, Malcolm could be pretty snobby sometimes. "Then quit sticking up for me."

But he knew, and I knew, I couldn't.

six

MARRYING MALCOLM MURGATROYD seemed like the worst punishment anybody could ever get. And I hadn't done anything to deserve it! Our parents thought it was cute, talking about Malcolm and me growing up and getting married. "A late bloomer," my mom called him. What I wanted to know was, how late? When was Malcolm going to bloom, and into what? I couldn't imagine him blooming into a Bruce Wyatt, or even a Dennis Duffy, ever, let alone in time to marry me.

But there was something else, something much, much worse than being promised to Malcolm Murgatroyd. It was something Mom and Dad didn't talk about. I forced myself never to think about it, but once in a while it would sort of hit me out of nowhere, like lightning.

When the doctors first discovered that Ian had muscular dystrophy, they did several tests, not only on Ian, but on Mom and Dad, too. Dr. Benedict explained that he was acting like a detective, trying to find out where the disease came from.

I was only seven and a half, but it seemed like a terribly bad idea to me. Who cared where it came from? What did he want to do, blame someone? And then, as if he thought I wasn't in the room, or was just too young to understand, he explained something to Mom. With his kind, serious eyes only meeting hers on every other word, he told her that it was possible that I, the "female child," might be a carrier of this type of MD. Mom cried and I remember feeling good that she was finally crying for me, like she cried for Ian; then I felt miserable for feeling good and I cried, too.

The next day I asked Malcolm what it meant to be a carrier and he said he thought it meant that someday my children might have what Ian had. At the time, this didn't really sink in; having children was something too far in the future. So I decided not to think about it, but it was always kind of a monster under the bed, and once in a while, like now, it would pop up and scare the heck out of me.

I did what I always did—I ignored the monster, and he went away and I busied myself with thinking about what a creep Malcolm Murgatroyd was for bringing his seal to school. I was thinking this on the way back to Miss Lindstrum's room; art would be over—no point in going back there. I took the long way back to class so I could pass by the special-ed room to say hi to Ian.

"Where ya goin'?" Malcolm asked, several steps behind.

I didn't answer.

"To see the alien leader?"

"To see my brother," I snapped. "I'm not part of that goof-o game of yours."

He scurried to catch up to me. The kid couldn't even run normally. "Yes you are! You're the Earth Princess, daughter of the Earth King. Our mission is to save you from the evil alien-destroyer ship. Ian's not an evil alien," he clarified. "He's a friendly one."

"Naturally."

The special-education classroom was in the school's main corridor, just past the gymnasium. Technically, Ian wasn't a special-ed student. But since he'd had his chair, on the days his class had P.E., Ian spent the hour in the special-ed room as a helper. It hadn't been his idea, not originally. At first, he would go to the gym or out on the playground with his class and watch them learn tumbling or run hurdles. That made him pretty miserable. So Miss Jacobs, the vice principal, suggested he use his P.E. time to help out in the special-ed class. I was pretty suspicious at first, wondering if this was just Miss Jacobs's way of getting Ian used to being around handicapped kids. And Ian—he *hated* the idea. But Miss Jacobs made a deal with him: all he had to do was try it once, and if he was uncomfortable, he could quit.

As it turned out, though, Ian wasn't uncomfortable at all. He loved helping the special-ed kids, and after the first day, he told Miss Jacobs he wouldn't quit for anything. She was really proud of him, and so was I. I also decided that Miss Jacobs was probably the smartest vice principal in the history of vice principals.

In the main corridor, I passed the gym and purposely did not look inside. I didn't want to see Ian's classmates learning to turn handsprings. I just didn't.

Malcolm was hot on my heels all the way to the special-ed room. I peeked in through the window of the door, feeling my throat dry up, and a strange dropping sensation in my stomach. The room had a weird effect on me. Those poor kids with helmets on and drooly faces, and wheelchairs—like Ian.

Miss Spalding (the sub who'd let Malcolm play kickball in third grade) waved to me. She wasn't a sub anymore; now she was the special-education teacher. I think she'd learned a lot between then and now. I think some of it she learned from us.

Anyway, she tapped Ian on the shoulder and motioned

for me to come in. At the sound of the door opening, all the special kids turned, except Timmy, who was hearing-impaired.

"Hello, Hannah."

"Hi, Miss Spalding." The room was bright and colorful, with toys everywhere. The other special-ed teacher, Mrs. Bellacristo, who looked like Mrs. Santa Claus, smiled at me. She was arranging cookies on a plate for snack time. A little girl in a wheelchair like Ian's was humming some happy tune. I was completely depressed.

"Whatcha want?" Ian asked, wheeling himself in my direction.

"Nothing. Just wanted to say hi."

"Hi."

"Hi."

For a moment I didn't know what else to say. Then there was the crash.

Everyone—even Timmy—jumped. Near the windows, a boy in a safety helmet was making an awful sound, something between crying and crowing, and he was jiggling and bouncing around. It looked like he was dancing. The crash had come from the pile of blocks he'd suddenly swept from the windowsill to the floor. Then, on purpose it seemed, he began banging his head against the wide sill.

"Oh, my . . ." I wanted to run, but somehow I felt frozen in place. Ian took my hand.

"It's okay. That's Jeffrey. He does this every once in a while."

Mrs. Bellacristo abandoned the cookies and hurried to Jeffrey. Miss Spalding was already beside him. I wondered why she just didn't throw her arms around him and tell him to stop it. Instead, she busied herself with moving things out of his path—especially the other children. Mrs. Bellacristo was speaking softly to Jeffrey, but I doubted very much he was listening. He just kept flinging himself around and banging his head.

"It's okay," Ian told me again, sounding like an older brother instead of a younger one. "But I think you should go."

I nodded and squeezed his hand, then backed slowly out of the classroom, leaving my brother in the middle of it. Miss Spalding was talking to Jeffrey now, too, and the girl in the other wheelchair was still humming away.

Malcolm was in the hall; he'd been watching from the door. He was about to say something to me, but as soon as the door closed behind me, I broke into a run. I ran hard, and only when I reached the metal emergency doors at the end of the corridor and burst out into the sunshine did I realize I was sobbing.

My knees seemed to crumble; I lowered myself to the grass. In a minute, Malcolm was there beside me.

"Don't cry, Hannah. It doesn't last long."

I looked up at him. "It lasts forever."

We were talking about two different things. Jeffrey's fit, or attack or whatever the special-ed teachers called it, was probably over already—that's what Malcolm meant. But the sickness, whatever it was, and the helmet—for Jeffrey and his family, those would last forever.

"I see what you mean," said Malcolm, sitting down in the grass beside me.

Oddly enough, I found myself thinking that the warm October sun would help to dry out poor Cecil. "I can't believe Ian has to be around that. It's so . . . pitiful." It hit me that I was crying more for Ian than for Jeffrey. "He's only nine years old. He shouldn't have to see that stuff. And Timmy . . . what is he? Six? And Jeffrey's older than us!" I laid back in the grass and closed my eyes. "It's all mixed up."

I felt the sun disappear behind a cloud. I thought of Cecil, without his fin. In some stuffed-animal world, was he now a candidate for special ed? It wasn't a funny thought—it wasn't supposed to be. It was just part of everything being mixed up.

I was still crying; the sun returned and I felt its brightness against my eyelids. Then I felt something soft and damp, like a soggy towel, against my hand. Malcolm's footsteps were swishes in the grass, then came the sound of the metal doors opening, closing. When I opened my eyes, I saw that Malcolm had left Cecil with me. I held it, the blind, one-legged seal. There in the sunshine I decided that Cecil might just need me as much as I, at that moment, needed him.

seven

"EVIE, TRADE WITH ME."

"Okay, what ya got?"

"Ham and cheese."

"Mustard?"

"Mayo."

"Good." She handed me her egg salad on rye.

"Thanks," I said, nibbling at the yellow mixture around the edges. "Evie, you're my best friend, right?"

"You know I am!" She shook her carton of chocolate milk. "Since the day I moved here. You were the only person who was nice to me from the start."

Around us, the cafeteria buzzed. Smells of peanut butter and tuna fish mingled in a pleasant, familiar way. I'd purposely selected an out-of-the-way table where Evie and I could talk.

"Do you think I'm too nice?" I asked, sipping my juice. "Too goody-goody?"

Evie shrugged. The blush had worn off more from her right cheek than from her left; she looked a little lopsided. "I think it's nice that you're nice. Except . . ."

I knew it. "Except what?"

"Except, I think you overdo it a bit when it comes to the Nerd Ball."

"Malcolm."

"Who else? I mean, I guess I feel sorry for him, too, but it's his problem. He's a geek, plain and simple, and geeks get picked on. That's just the way it goes."

I frowned. "Maybe it shouldn't go like that."

Evie was chomping into what had formerly been my sandwich. "It probably shouldn't. That's your goody-goody opinion. But, Hannah, let's face it. The cool kids have a lot of responsibilities. It's our responsibility to set fashion trends, decide what music to like and rough up the nerds now and then."

For the first time, Evie was making me mad. "You think it's our responsibility to torment Malcolm? Evie, that's a rotten thing to say."

"Rotten maybe, but true." She swallowed and shrugged. "At least we give Murgadope a break once in a while." Then she asked, as if she'd been wondering forever, "Why do you always stick up for him, Hannah? I mean, *always*?"

I bit into my sandwich. I was stalling.

Evie was waiting. "Why, Hannah?"

I decided to start with the standard response. "Because Ian likes him." The egg salad hit my stomach like a bomb. "Because he's nice to Ian."

But by now that was common knowledge. No one had ever said it to my face, but I'd heard them whispering about it. They saw Malcolm Murgatroyd as a misfit and it was perfectly natural for him to pal around with other misfits at school—a third-grader in a wheelchair, for instance. That was acceptable. And they couldn't really hold it against me if I felt the need to stick up for him, sort of a trade-off for him treating Ian nicely. As far as everyone else was concerned, that was the extent of my relationship with Malcolm.

Evie, on the other hand, knew me well enough to know

that I was holding something back now, and that something was the real answer to the mystery of me and Malcolm. She leaned over the table a little farther. "And . . . ?"

I drew a deep breath and decided to tell her the truth. After all, she was my best friend. "Promise me you won't tell anyone if I tell you the reason."

She nodded, her eyes wide.

"Okay. Well, it's not just because Malcolm is nice to Ian at school. There's more, actually. It has to do with family loyalty."

Evie gasped. "Don't tell me you and Malcolm are related!"

"No! Not exactly. But we did grow up together."

She cocked an eyebrow. "Exactly how together?"

"Very together. Like since we were born." I sighed. "You'd never believe it, but Malcolm's parents are completely cool. His mom used to be an almost famous dancer and she's like really beautiful. And his dad! His dad is super cute, and he's a doctor. He's even a jock! He played football with my dad in college."

Evie slurped her milk. "And these two perfect people have a son with gigantic teeth and greasy hair and bargain-basement sneakers?"

"Weird, isn't it?" I started on my corn chips. "But it's true. Anyway, my parents and Malcolm's parents have all been best friends since forever and ever." I leaned across the table and whispered, "We go on vacation together every summer!"

"You're kidding! You've actually seen him in a bathing suit?" Evie bit her lip; she had an even worse thought. "And he's seen you in a bathing suit?" She shuddered. "Gross."

"There's more," I told her, referring to but not ready to mention the fact that my parents expected me to marry him. I shrugged. "But mostly it's because of Ian's disease."

Evie—and most of my friends—had a way of looking

around, or down or up or just somewhere else, whenever the subject of Ian's illness came up. It made them very uncomfortable, I knew, because they were always scared they'd say the wrong thing. I didn't blame them; sometimes even I didn't know what to say. Evie's eyes appeared to be glued to her Ring-Ding.

"Malcolm is very special to Ian. Probably because Malcolm doesn't have any friends, he's more sensitive or something. Like, when Ian got the wheelchair this summer"—I paused to crunch a chip and shake my head—"even my mom and dad were confused. But Malcolm took over. He helped Ian learn to drive it, and back up, and he even invented a game about aliens to make Ian feel less, you know, self-conscious about it." Self-conscious was the word Ian's doctor had used: try not to make him feel self-conscious about it. Yeah, right. But Malcolm was as smooth as silk.

"So that's why you stick up for Malcolm? Because he's Ian's friend and you grew up together?" Evie looked like she respected this. Not like she herself planned to be any nicer to Malcolm because of it, but like she kind of understood my point.

"We're *still* growing up together," I said, sighing. "Can we keep this just between us?"

She smiled. "You think I'd want anyone to know I'm best friends with someone who goes on vacation with a nerd?"

I smiled back. "I guess you wouldn't."

She bit into her Ring-Ding. "Did you see Bruce Wyatt doing push-ups in gym? Oooh, baby!" We giggled over Bruce for the rest of the period.

eight

I plunked my schoolbooks down on the hall table and followed the sound of voices to the patio. "Mom?"

"Out here, Hannah."

I knew, from the car in the driveway, that Kate was visiting. On my way through the family room, then the kitchen, I went over in my mind what I planned to mention to Kate about Malcolm's hair.

"Hi!" I kissed my mom. She poured me a glass of iced tea from the pitcher. "Thanks. Hi, Kate."

"Hi, sweetheart."

Kate was too pretty to be somebody's mom. Especially Malcolm's. My mom was pretty, too, but Kate just had this look—the look of a ballerina, which she'd been before she married Dr. Steve. Kate was slender and fair, with long, shining blond hair.

Hair. That reminded me . . . "Kate, what kind of shampoo do you use?"

She touched her bangs, smiling. "Oh, no special kind. Whatever's on sale."

That figured. "Oh, I was just wondering." I made a little fuss of running my fingers through my own hair, which, I'd been told, was one of my best features. "I'm thinking of switching brands because my hair feels a little greasy lately."

My mom, who's a personal-hygiene fanatic, looked horrified. "What?" She stroked my hair. "It's not in the least bit greasy, Hannah!" she said, which was the truth.

"Well, not greasy, I guess, but maybe just a little oily. They do have shampoo especially for oily hair, don't they?" I directed my question to Kate, hoping it might strike a chord regarding Malcolm, whose hair truly was oily. "Ishy," as Sheila McElroy had so brilliantly called it.

"Yes, they do."

"Is that kind of shampoo ever on sale?" I asked, trying to sound offhand.

The moms exchanged glances. "What are you getting at, kiddo?" asked mine, her iced-tea glass poised at her lips.

I took a long swallow of my tea, trying to think of a polite way to say it. "The kids were laughing at Malcolm's hair today," I blurted. "Sheila said it was oily. Maybe there's some shampoo for oily hair on sale somewhere that could dry it up some." I looked quickly from my mother to Kate. "Just a suggestion."

Kate smiled again. "Thank you, Hannah. It's a very good suggestion."

I thought she'd be angry—at the very least, insulted—when I told her her son was a slime-head, slick-hair greaser. But she wasn't. She was glad. And she knew I was just trying to help.

"As a matter of fact," my mother was saying, "I've got a bottle of shampoo for oily hair upstairs. I bought it by mistake. Kate can take it home for Malcolm tonight."

I sat with them awhile, until we heard Ian's bus pull up. He rode a special bus—it was half the length of mine, and had an elevator thing, a platform that lifted and lowered him in his chair. We could hear the driver opening the big door and setting up the platform.

Mom excused herself to go meet Ian at the bus stop. That left Kate and me alone.

"Malcolm appreciates the way you look out for him, Hannah," she said suddenly. "And so do I."

"No problem," I told her. But it was a problem. I was getting tired of it. "I wouldn't have to look out for him so much, though, if he'd just try to fit in a little better." I said it before I could stop myself.

Kate nodded. She was smiling, but it was a different smile than before. It was a sad smile. "Malcolm is different. Fitting in is not his specialty."

You're telling me, I thought.

She tapped one of her pretty polished nails against her glass. "His specialty is fitting out, so to speak. Do you see?"

I didn't.

"Fitting out. With Ian, for example. Now, I know the other children aren't mean to Ian, like they are to Malcolm"—the sadness spread from her smile to her eyes—"but they don't exactly make an effort to be around him, do they?"

I thought of Ian's friend T.J. from down the street. I don't think T.J. had been at our house more than twice since the wheelchair. According to Ian, T.J. was the fastest runner in the third grade, something I knew Ian would have given anything to be. I felt my cheeks getting hot. All of a sudden, I was mad.

"Malcolm 'fits out' with Ian. Honestly, they're like brothers."

I nodded. "Ian needs Malcolm. It's weird, it's like Malcolm has this"—I searched for the word—"talent for cheering up Ian. Like he's got some kind of gift for handling special kids."

"In many ways, Malcolm is special himself."

Kate was right. It wasn't just a kid's mother talking, either. Malcolm *was* special; I'd said so myself to Evie at lunch. He bugged me and he was a nerd and all, but I had to admit it,

Malcolm was special. "We saw one of the special-ed kids have an attack today," I told Kate. "And Malcolm wasn't even scared."

Kate nodded, sipping her tea.

"Here we are!" Mom called, pushing Ian up the slate path to the patio.

"Hey, Wheels!" Kate called. That was her nickname for Ian. He loved it almost as much as the alien game.

"Hi, Kate."

Bounding around the side of the house came Celeste and Olivia Murgatroyd, the twins. They were a year older than Ian, two years younger than me, and they had their mother's good looks. "We rode Ian's bus," Celeste declared proudly. "We told the principal you'd be here and he gave us permission."

My mom was pouring iced tea for them. "It was neat," cried Olivia, taking a seat.

"Yeah!" echoed Celeste. "I never rode the retard bus before!" Her face tightened instantly, tears bubbling up in her eyes. "Oh gosh, I'm sorry, Ian. I didn't mean . . ."

My mother was looking away, toward her rosebushes. She was trying not to be upset.

Kate looked uncomfortable, and now Olivia, too, was crying.

"We're sorry, Ian," Olivia said. "She didn't mean to call it that."

What we need now, I was thinking, is Malcolm.

But Ian was not upset, or if he was, he didn't show it. "Don't feel bad, Celeste." He used the controls of his chair to maneuver himself right up to her seat. "I know everyone calls it the retard bus. I used to call it that, too. Honest, I don't mind."

The look Celeste gave him was one of pure adoration and love, and relief. I felt a lump welling up in my throat. Good boy, Ian, I thought. I remembered them, Celeste and Ian and Olivia, in the wading pool together when they were babies. Six little legs, tanned and pudgy around the knees. Six good legs. I closed my eyes and let the moment flood back to me —the sun, the sound of sandpipers, and a song Kate used to sing. A song Ian loved. I tried to remember the words— something about sunshine—but the hideous echo of "retard bus" came rolling back across my thoughts like a wave on the sand.

"Let me run up and grab that shampoo before I forget," Mom said, leaving the table, and I knew she was remembering, too.

The retard bus.

I sat up in bed for a long time, thinking about how I used to call it that. The small bus with the elevator platform and the seat belts, the special-ed bus. How could I have ever called it that, I wondered now. The words left a bad taste in my mouth.

Quietly, I got out of bed and tiptoed into the hall. A nightlight was glowing in my yellow bathroom. In that light, my shadow was tall and odd-looking, rippling in the flowery folds of the shower curtain. I took a long drink of water, but the words still stuck on my tongue. "The retard bus," I whispered, hoping they would vanish if I said them out loud.

On the first day of school, only five weeks ago, the special-ed bus had stopped at our corner for the first time. Mom, Dad, and Malcolm stood outside with Ian; they'd hooked his backpack over the chair handle, and he was wearing brand-new sneakers.

I squirmed, thinking that now, five weeks later, Ian's sneakers still looked brand-new.

I'd watched from the kitchen window as the bus driver came out and introduced himself. He was a nice man with very little hair. He'd helped Ian maneuver the chair onto the platform and set the thing in motion. Behind her back, my mom was wringing her hands. I think I held my breath. Vaguely, through the dusty bus windows, I could see the shapes of the other students on Ian's bus. That was the day it became "Ian's bus" instead of the retard bus.

"I'll ride the bus with you, Ian," Malcolm had said the night before, when we had our annual Last Day of Vacation Barbecue at the Murgatroyds' house. "We can recruit some of the other kids for our alien game! That headgear and those helmets! Talk about aliens!" Everyone knew Malcolm wasn't being mean.

Ian was buttering an ear of corn; his chair was pushed up close to the redwood picnic table. "Cool! Mom, can Malcolm ride the bus with me tomorrow?"

"I imagine we'd have to have permission," my mother said, passing a basket of hot-dog buns to Olivia. "It's too late to request now."

Ian looked disappointed and I wondered if my parents were angry because I hadn't offered to ride the bus with my brother. I had my reasons, and right then those reasons were giving me a stomachache. I passed on potato salad.

"Well, I can wait at the stop with you!" Malcolm blurted. There were kernels of corn stuck in his teeth and butter glistening on his chin. "I can wait at your stop until you get on the new bus, and then get on my bus with Hannah, 'cause, after all, that is my bus. I don't think you need permission to get on your own bus at a different spot."

I leaned against the vanity in my pretty bathroom. Malcolm had called it "the new bus." Not the retard bus. I ran the cold water and splashed some on my face. How come Malcolm knew everything?

But I still didn't want to marry him.

nine

"OKAY, SO WE'VE GOT ME, you, Sheila, Casey, Ashley Pe-rillo, Ashley Wells, Kimberly, and Lynn." Evie made a check beside every name on her list. "Those are the girls."

I grinned. "No kidding."

She continued down the list. "Bruce, Dennis, Eddie, Todd, Scott, Anthony, Alex Delaney, and Alex Gold."

"The boys."

Evie was planning the first boy-girl party in the history of Morningside Elementary. We were sitting on her bed, final-izing the details.

When she'd announced to me, almost a month ago, "For my birthday, I'm going to have a boy-girl slumber party!" my eyes had gone completely round.

"Boys are going to sleep over?" I'd tried not to sound horrified, but if Bruce Wyatt ever saw me in my pajamas, I'd die.

"Not exactly," she'd admitted. "It's a regular boy-girl party till nine o'clock. Then the boys go home and the girls sleep over and talk about them."

"Great!" A boy-girl non-slumber party was still pretty ex-citing, as far as I was concerned.

We decided we had to be very particular about the boys

we invited, so Evie and I wrote up a questionnaire to circulate
to the girls.

Questionnaire about Evie Neville's
Boy-Girl Slumber Party

Name: _____

1. Can you come? YES   NO   (circle one)
2. Write the names of three boys that you like. Circle
the one you like best.

_____

_____

_____

3. Do you think the B.G.S.P. should have dancing?
YES   NO   (circle one)
Please fill this out and return to Evie or Hannah.

DON'T SHOW ANYONE!!!

Love,
Evie and Hannah

We were standing in line for the photocopy machine at
the town library when Bruce spotted us.

"Hi. Whatcha copying?"

"Nothing," we said together. I shifted my weight and the
pile of change in my pocket jingled. I was holding the original
questionnaire because Evie's hands were always clammy and
we didn't want it to wrinkle.

"C'mon," said Bruce, smiling. "What is it?"

I smiled back to distract him. It worked. "What are you doing here?" I asked.

"Me and Den are working on our autobiographies. Wanna sit with us?"

The man in front of us finished his copying, and Evie shoved me toward the machine. "Sure," she said. "We'll be right there."

Bruce went to join Dennis, and Evie stood lookout while I slipped enough coins for six copies into the copier. The machine started with a sound that reminded me of Ian's wheelchair; from under the cover, a green light flashed six times. I took the six copies from the out-tray.

"Done!"

Evie put the copies in a folder, which she tucked into her looseleaf binder, and then shoved her binder into her book bag. "Dennis Duffy has the most incredible green eyes!" she whispered as we headed off to find him and Bruce. All of a sudden, I knew whose name Evie was going to circle!

On the way home, Evie wanted to stop at the drugstore to see if they'd gotten any new makeup. A little bell on the door announced our arrival; Mr. Stanpool looked up from the counter and smiled at us.

"How do you like this?" asked Evie, holding up a tester of Mad About Melon lip gloss.

"It's orange," I said, wrinkling my nose.

"No it's not, it's Mad About Melon." She held the tester to her lips.

"Cooties!" I warned. You could never be sure who'd been testing the testers. Evie stopped short of her mouth and made a gooey swipe of Mad About Melon across the back of her hand instead. "Not bad," I told her.

The lip gloss was $5.95 and between us (since we'd used

most our change to copy the questionnaire) we only had $1.70, which was enough for a Milky Way and a pack of gum. We were arguing over peppermint or strawberry when the little bell rang and Bruce appeared.

He saw us right away. "Hey," he teased. "Quit following me." Bruce went to the magazine rack and grabbed a couple of comic books and a *Sports Illustrated.*

"Hi, Mr. Stanpool," I said, placing the items on the counter.

"Hello, Hannah." He rang up the candy and the gum.

Bruce came up behind us and put the magazines down. "Man, that autobiography is a real pain."

"You can say that again," agreed Evie.

Bruce rolled his eyes. "Knowing Lindstrum, she'll make us read them out loud, too. Man, I hate hearing everybody read junk out loud. It's so stupid. I wish she didn't . . ." Bruce spotted something on the counter and stopped midsentence, just as Evie was handing Mr. Stanpool our money. I followed Bruce's gaze to a canister beside the cash register. The canister was covered in white paper with the words JERRY'S KIDS printed in a blue arc. Below the words was a picture of Jerry Lewis looking very serious and concerned, and a little boy with braces on his legs. At the bottom was written HELP STOP MUSCULAR DYSTROPHY.

Evie saw it, too. Mr. Stanpool had given her twelve cents' change and she hesitated. Then she dropped the dime and two pennies through the slit in the top of the canister. The change made a dull jingle when it landed on the other dimes and pennies and quarters that had been donated.

Bruce dug into his pocket and pulled out three quarters. He reached over and plunked them in, but he drew his hand away too quickly and toppled the canister. The coins inside jangled loudly, like an alarm. Bruce looked embarrassed, and

I could tell that Evie was uncomfortable. Mr. Stanpool remained focused on the dollar bills in the drawer of the register.

"It's okay," I said, taking charge and standing the canister up again. The money settled at the bottom with a metallic thump. It was not unlike the sound of Ian's silverware hitting the kitchen floor, when his muscles turned on him and he suddenly couldn't keep his grip on a fork or a spoon. I was familiar with the sound; it had been happening a lot lately. Then, because nobody knew what to say, I swallowed hard and said, "Thanks. That was nice of you." After all, the money in the can was mine, in a way.

"We'd better go," said Evie, snatching up the Milky Way and the gum. "C'mon."

"See ya," said Bruce.

"See ya."

The blue-and-white image of Jerry Lewis stared out at me from the canister. I wanted to tell him that there was eighty-seven cents in there that was to be applied solely to research regarding the condition of a certain Ian Billings, age nine.

ten

Six copies of the B.G.S.P. Questionnaire went out; seven came back. The seventh one was the original, which I'd stupidly left on the glass of the copier, and which Bruce and Dennis must have nabbed when Evie and I left the library.

And which they filled out with the help of every boy in our class.

Evie and I sat at the secluded lunch table again, reviewing the seventh questionnaire.

Questionnaire about Evie Neville's
Boy-Girl Slumber Party

Name: *Hannah Billings*

1. Can you come? (YES) NO   (circle one)
2. Write the names of three boys that you like. Circle the one you like best.

Malcolm Murgatroyd
Malcolm Murgatroyd
Malcolm Murgatroyd

3. Do you think the B.G.S.P. should have dancing?
(YES) NO (circle one) *with Malcolm Murgatroyd!*
Please fill this out and return to Evie or Hannah.

DON'T SHOW ANYONE!!!

Love,
Evie and Hannah

It was a rotten joke, and the joke was on me. But I couldn't help thinking I deserved it a little for being dumb enough to leave the original in the copier.

"Whose handwriting is that?" Evie asked, squinting at the page. "I don't think it's Dennis's."

I shrugged. "Who cares who *wrote* it? They all did it together. They think I'm a nerd lover." There was a knot in my stomach and my eyes were stinging.

"You can't blame them, really," replied Evie softly.

"I guess not. But I thought Bruce was supposed to like me."

Evie crumpled up the questionnaire and stuffed it in her empty lunch bag. "He does like you, and you know it! The boys were just being . . . well, you know . . . boys. That's a synonym for jerks. Besides, it was more of a joke on Malcolm than you. They love to pick on Malcolm. Don't take it so hard, Hannah. It was just a joke."

That made me feel a little better. But only a little.

eleven

ONCE EVIE FINALIZED her guest list, it was time to start planning. She handed me half of the stack of invitations, which I filled out with the date and time of the party and her phone number. I was filling out the girls' invitations, which is why I was allowed to include the Nevilles' phone number. Evie was not about to supply her number to the boys; they could RSVP in school.

"Except Dennis," she giggled. "I'm writing my number on Dennis's invitation."

"What about food?" I wondered out loud. "We should be careful not to serve anything that gives bad breath, or makes you burp." I would never forgive myself if I burped in front of Bruce.

Evie thought for a minute. "Nothing stinky, nothing burpy." She frowned. "That's just about everything! Mexican cheese chips, onion dip, soda!"

I frowned, too. "We have to serve soda."

Evie bit her lip, thinking. "The boys can burp themselves silly, for all I care," she said. "We'll have soda for them and iced tea for us!"

That sounded okay to me. "And we can eat plain potato chips with no dip." Evie nodded. "Besides, those Mexican chips turn your fingers orange."

"Do you think Dennis will get me a present?" Evie asked suddenly. "Not that he has to, but it would be nice, ya know? My first present from a boy?"

I wished I could say the same thing if Bruce ever bought me a present, but I'd been getting birthday presents from Malcolm for years. Kate picked them out, I was sure—on *sale*, I was even more sure. But the cards always read "Love, Malcolm."

Gross.

"This is going to be a cool party, Evie," I said, shaking the thought. I licked the last envelope and flopped back on Evie's bed. "A real cool party."

Evie's mom picked me up for school the next morning; we wanted to get in early to distribute the invitations.

Miss Lindstrum wasn't in the classroom yet. That was a good thing, because she had a rule about not passing out party invitations unless you were inviting every single kid in the class, which never happened. So I'd have to work fast, and sneak the invitations into the desks before Miss Lindstrum arrived.

I felt bad, because I didn't like breaking rules on purpose. And I happened to agree that this particular rule was a good one, because the kids who didn't get an invitation were bound to feel crummy and left out. But I was just so excited about Evie's party. It was an uncomfortable coincidence that, as I was thinking this, I was walking right by Malcolm's desk, and very much *not* slipping an invitation into it. I made a promise to myself to be extra-good about trying not to break rules for the rest of the day—sort of like extra credit.

I had just finished putting Bruce Wyatt's invitation inside his desk when I heard Miss Lindstrum in the hall. I ran to my own seat, whipped out my library book, and was pretending to be totally lost in Chapter 4 when the teacher came in.

"Good morning, Hannah," she said, heading for her desk. "You're in early!"

I just smiled.

She sat down at her desk. "I've been meaning to ask you, dear," she said gently. "How is your little brother getting along?"

"The wheelchair is a big adjustment," I said, repeating what I'd heard my mom say a hundred times. Then I grinned. "He likes to pretend he's riding in an alien spaceship."

Miss Lindstrum smiled again. "The special-education teachers say he seems to be in good spirits, considering."

Considering, I thought. Considering that good old T.J. is the fastest runner in the third grade and Ian isn't, never was, never will be. "He gets upset sometimes," I told the teacher. She was looking right at me during this conversation, unlike my friends. It was nice, for a change.

I went back to pretending to read my library book until a few more kids showed up.

In a while, the boys were meeting in their corner, talking about the party. When Malcolm arrived from his monitor duty, the boys started to crack up and then Bruce said, "Shhhhh," and Dennis said, "Cool it!" and they just giggled quietly, looking over their shoulders at Malcolm.

I spent the weekend working on my autobiography. "The Hannah Billings Story," I called it. Ian said it sounded like the title for the autobiography of a famous baseball player.

Starting the project was easy. There wasn't much to tell about being a baby. Then I got to the part in my life I could actually remember, and things got complicated.

"Shoot!" I dropped my pencil on the desk and rested my chin in my hands.

"What's wrong, Hannah?" Dad asked.

"Dad, is there such thing as a fiction autobiography?"

He laughed. "No. Fiction is make-believe," he explained. "An autobiography is real. It's the true story of your life."

"That's what I was afraid of."

"You're afraid of telling the truth about your life?"

I picked up the pencil and gnawed on the eraser. "Parts of it."

Dad looked surprised, but all he said was "Take the pencil out of your mouth," and left.

The parts I was afraid of telling, of course, were the parts that included Malcolm. What if Miss Lindstrum made us read the reports out loud to the class? She was notorious for that. The problem was, most of my childhood memories included Dr. Steve and Kate and Malcolm and the twins. Vacations at the shore, barbecues in the summer, sled riding at Rolling Hills Country Club in the winter. It had been pretty difficult finding snapshots that didn't include at least one Murgatroyd.

"When I was five," I wrote, "my parents and I went on vacation to the shore and stayed in a cottage on the beach." I paused, chewing the eraser again. "Absolutely no one came with us. It was just me, my mom and dad, and my brother Ian, who was just a baby. Nobody from this town or this school came along and stayed in the upstairs of the cottage."

But all the good pictures of the shore had Malcolm in them. I got this great idea about cutting the snapshots up (cutting Malcolm *out*, to be exact) and making a collage, but Mom had a fit about that. She loved those pictures exactly the way they were. So I was stuck with a few shots in which Malcolm was looking the other way, or badly focused, or so covered in white sunblock gook and long sleeves and sun hats that no one would recognize him. Still, the choice was limited. So much for extra credit.

I worked on the autobiography all day. Around dusk, I got

to the part in my life when we discovered that Ian had muscular dystrophy. I guess I was sitting there in the dark for a while, because Mom came into the study and turned on the desk lamp. I was leaning over my notebook, thinking—thinking, but not seeing a word on the page in the shadowy light.

"How's it going?" Mom asked softly, and I jumped.

"Not bad. I just got to the MD."

Mom sat on the arm of Dad's leather chair, the one he always said he'd smoke his pipe in if he smoked a pipe. "I guess that's a pretty difficult chapter to write."

I nodded. "It hurts when I have to think about it all at once. It brings it back."

"I know, honey."

"He's just a little kid, Mom," I said, noticing the change in my voice. "He could be faster than T.J., I bet if only . . ." But there was no point in saying it. "His sneakers . . ." A big tear splashed down on the page in front of me and smeared the "s" in "dystrophy." For a minute, I thought I could cry all over the page and wipe out the entire word, both words, and make the whole thing go away, vanish in a gray, number-2 lead puddle on my homework. Or I could erase it with my chewed-up eraser. I rubbed my eyes. "His sneakers should at least be *dirty* by now."

Mom reached out and stroked my hair. She didn't say anything.

Neither did I, for a long moment. I didn't want to admit that I'd actually considered not writing about it at all, just leaving it out. As it was, I was already leaving out most of my childhood by leaving out the Murgatroyds. If I left out the MD, my autobiography might as well have been about somebody else.

I heard Ian clunking into the television in the family room. Mom laughed. "He's a pretty crazy driver, huh?"

"Slow down, you nut!" I called toward the family room and Ian responded with a loud wet raspberry. I laughed, too.

"I think you've done enough homework for one Saturday," Mom said, patting my shoulder. "Maybe you should put it away for now."

I nodded, and closed the notebook on my autobiography, catching a glimpse of the first sentence. "I am Hannah Billings," it read.

"I guess I should," I said, but I wondered, snapping off the desk lamp, how do you put away your life.

twelve

I WORKED ON MY AUTOBIOGRAPHY on and off all week. That weekend Mom took me shopping for Evie's gift. Ian needed some stuff for his Halloween costume, so he came, too. It was only his second time at the mall in his wheelchair. Mom was pushing him—or driving him, as Ian called it. I was uncomfortable to notice that little kids stared at him. Even a few dopey grownups. What's the matter? I wanted to yell. Haven't you ever seen a kid in a wheelchair before? It didn't take me long to perfect a dirty look that said as much, but I stopped using it when it occurred to me that maybe—just maybe—they hadn't. So I concentrated on thinking of something terrific to get Evie for her birthday.

"Let's try the Giggling Giant!" I suggested.

Ian looked at me funny. "What the heck is a giggling giant?"

"A big guy in a good mood," I teased.

"It's a clothing store," my mom said, tousling his hair.

Ian rolled his eyes. "Great."

The mall was empty for a Saturday. I hurried toward the Giggling Giant, secretly planning a new outfit for myself along with Evie's birthday gift.

The salesgirls made a point of looking away from Ian. No one asked my mom if she was shopping for anything in particular. The store manager kept her eyes glued to the register when the handle of Ian's wheelchair caught in the sleeve of a sweater hanging on a rack and brought down an entire pile of silk scarves arranged on the top tier.

"Oops, sorry," said Mom, to everyone and no one. Ian's jaw was set. I hurried to the back of the store.

Mom stayed pretty still after the sweater incident, and I browsed until I found the perfect gift for Evie: a really cool purse and a matching makeup case. I also found a new shirt for myself to wear to the party. I knew I wouldn't get an argument from Mom; she was acting very anxious because one of the salesgirls was fixing up the scarves and looking disgusted. I figured Mom would just want to get out of there, and wouldn't bother to make a fuss about me getting the new shirt.

Something flickered through me, some kind of realization that getting the shirt under these conditions wasn't right. I handed Evie's purse to the woman at the register and almost decided against the shirt, but I couldn't help myself. The sound of Ian's chair buzzing (he'd found an aisle wide enough to navigate through) sent the flicker straight to my stomach.

"Will you be taking the shirt as well?" the woman asked.

I handed it to her. "Yes."

As expected, Mom didn't say a word, just handed over the money.

Ian was waiting for us at the entrance to the store. He looked proud about driving himself out without any major collisions.

I hung my shopping bag on one of the handles of the chair, then immediately plucked it off and carried it myself.

"Look," said Ian. We were passing through the cosmetics department in Lord and Taylor. "It's Malcolm."

"Malcolm? What's he doing in the makeup department?" He appeared to be just wandering, to tell the truth, but he was carrying a little bag. He'd bought something.

"Kate's birthday isn't for months," Mom observed.

"Malcolm! Hey, Malcolm!" Ian steered himself toward Malcolm, who shoved the bag behind his back as soon as he saw us.

"Howdy!"

"Whatcha doin' in the beauty section?" Ian asked.

Malcolm swallowed. "Nothing. I'm lost. I was looking for the exit."

"We're on our way out," my mother told him. "Follow us."

"I need the exit where the bus stop is."

"Don't be silly," said Mom. "We'll drive you home."

Malcolm's big ears went pink. "Thanks."

I was clutching the handles of my shopping bag so tight they made marks in my palms. The mall was always crawling with kids from school—Bruce and Dennis came to browse the sporting-goods stores and record shops at least twice a week. I didn't want anyone to spot me with the sixth-grade geekmaster.

"Let Malcolm drive the spaceship, Mom!"

Malcolm took control and wheeled off a few feet ahead of us, he and Ian making bleeping noises and speaking their made-up alien language to each other.

I must have looked pale or scared or something because Mom asked, "Are you all right?"

"I need the ladies' room," I said, spotting the "Rest Rooms" sign. "I'll meet you at the car, okay?"

Mom frowned. "You know I don't like you wandering

around the mall by yourself. And definitely not the parking lot!"

I crossed my legs and bounced a little to let her know how urgently I had to go (which I didn't). Malcolm and Ian were almost to the exit.

"I'll pull the car up," she said, fishing in her purse for the keys. "I'll meet you right outside those doors."

I nodded and hurried off in the direction of the ladies' lounge.

"If you're not out in five minutes," Mom called after me, "I'm sending Malcolm in to find you!"

In that case, I thought, I'll be out in four.

The ladies' room in Lord and Taylor looked like somebody's living room. There were ornate light fixtures and plush chairs, which clashed with the beat-up pay phone on the wall. Since I didn't actually have to go, I just put my bag down and leaned against the counter to wait. Behind me, a toilet flushed. The pink metal door swung open and in the mirror I saw Sheila McElroy emerge from the stall.

"Hi, Hannah!"

"Oh, hi, Sheila."

She flipped on the faucet and pumped some soap into her hand. "Hey," she said, noticing my shopping bag. "I love the Giggling Giant! What did you get?"

"A birthday present for Evie. A real cool purse. And I got a shirt to wear to the party."

"Let's see!" She was holding her hands under the hot-air dryer, so she had to shout when she said, "Nice purse!" and "Great shirt!" But she didn't sound as if she meant it.

I folded the shirt quickly and stuffed it back in the bag. It had to be almost two minutes already, and I didn't want Malcolm to come tracking me down.

"I was shopping for Evie, too," said Sheila, "but I couldn't find anything I thought she'd like."

"Oh," I said. I was trying to think of a way to get out of there fast . . . two and a half minutes and counting! My hand was on the doorknob.

"How are you getting home?" she asked, moving toward the pay phone in the corner. "I'm calling my mom to pick me up, if you need a ride."

"Thanks, but my mom's here. She's getting the car and meeting me at the exit."

"Oh." Sheila put the phone back on its hook. "Then can I get a ride with you?"

Ordinarily, I would have said "Sure, fine," but today, with our extra passenger—no chance.

"Well, um . . ." Four minutes. I hoped they had some trouble getting Ian's wheelchair in the trunk, which would give me some more time, and then I heard myself saying, "I'm sorry, Sheila, but . . . see, we've got the small car today, and it's pretty cramped, you know, with the wheelchair."

The wheelchair. It was like a magic word.

"Sure," she said quickly. "I understand. No problem. My mom was planning to come get me anyhow." She reached into her pocket for a coin. "I'll just call her."

"Bye, Sheila," I said, stepping through the door.

I felt like a creep. It was the second time that afternoon that Ian's chair had gotten me what I wanted.

I followed the main aisle of Lord and Taylor to the exit. Through the glass doors, I could see Mom's car at the curb. Ian was in the front seat, and Malcolm was in the back. As always, the wheelchair was folded up and out of the way in the trunk. There was plenty of room for Sheila. My head hurt.

When I reached the sidewalk, Malcolm leaned over and opened the car door for me.

That was when I heard Sheila calling, "Hannah, wait up! You forgot your bag!"

I whirled around; Sheila was out of breath from hurrying to catch me. She was holding my Giggling Giant shopping bag.

"Thanks," I said, praying she wouldn't notice Malcolm, or the absence of the chair in the backseat.

But she purposely kept her eyes low; I guess she didn't want to look at Ian. She didn't see Malcolm. She didn't see my mom's window going down, either; Mom was about to offer her a ride.

"See you in school, Hannah," she said, and darted back into Lord and Taylor, her outline shimmying in the glass as the mall door swung slowly closed.

I tossed my bag into the car and hopped in after it. I looked around. "Where's Malcolm?"

"Right here." His muffled voice came from beneath an old blanket that my mom kept under the seat. Malcolm himself was practically under the seat, squeezed in on the floor. "Is the coast clear?"

Mom pulled out into the parking lot and I said, "Yeah. The coast is clear."

He tossed the blanket off his head, then stuffed it back under the seat and popped up from the floor.

I suppose I should have thanked him for hiding. But I didn't. I was thinking how rotten I felt for taking advantage —indirectly, but still taking advantage—of Ian's disease.

One glance at my mother in the rearview mirror told me she was furious; her eyebrows were knit low and her mouth was set in an angry line. The look made me instantly miserable. I tried to cheer myself up with a peek at my new shirt, but when I saw it, rumpled up in the shopping bag, I knew I wasn't going to be wearing it to Evie's party. Or anywhere. For some reason, all of a sudden, I hated that shirt.

thirteen

ALL EVIE AND I COULD THINK ABOUT was her party. We even decided we weren't going to go trick-or-treating on Halloween. We agreed that it was kid stuff and anyone planning a boy-girl slumber party was certainly too mature for trick or treat.

On Halloween night, after Dad drove Ian, in his alien makeup, over to Malcolm's house, Mom drove me over to Evie's. Around seven, we started nibbling on the mini-Butterfingers her mother had bought. At 7:20, we started on the Snickers bars. And at a quarter to eight, Evie got such a craving for a Milky Way that we threw on a couple of her sister's old dance-recital costumes and went trick-or-treating after all.

Mrs. Neville drove me home around nine. When I walked in, my parents were checking Ian's trick-or-treat candy and Ian was munching on what was left of the 3 Musketeers bars my mom had been giving out.

"How was it, Ian?" I asked, sitting down at the kitchen table.

"Inconvenient."

That was Malcolm's word, I was sure. "What do you mean?"

He bit into a chocolate bar. "Porch steps."

"Oh." I hadn't thought of that.

"A couple people came down from the porch and put candy in my bag. Most of them just gave extra stuff to Malcolm and told him to give it to me." He shrugged. "All I know is, I got tons of candy."

"I'll say," said Mom, sweeping it off the table and back into the bag.

Ian took his parent-approved goodies and wheeled off and Mom said she was going to find some cold cream to remove his alien makeup. That left my father and me at the kitchen table. He was looking out the window.

"What are you thinking about, Dad?" I asked.

His voice was thoughtful and sad when he answered. "Porch steps, Hannah. I'm thinking about porch steps."

The leaves had been bursting like red-and-gold fireworks against the sky all through October, but on the second Saturday of November, the day of Evie's party, I woke up to find the grass blanketed with leaves.

"Well," said Ian at breakfast, strumming his fingers on the armrests of the wheelchair, "at least I won't have to do the raking this year." He grinned at me.

"Raking's not so bad," I said brightly, finishing my waffles. "It's good exercise and I'll get lots of fresh air, and . . ."

"And Bruce Wyatt called yesterday and offered to come over and rake the yard for five dollars," Mom finished for me.

I blushed. "Oh yeah." I couldn't keep from smiling. "I forgot."

"Tell this Wyatt kid I want that lawn spotless when he's done." Dad sounded gruff, but I could see him trying to mask his own smile behind his coffee cup. "He's coming here to rake, not to flirt!"

"Dad!"

"I mean it, Hannah," said Dad, shaking a piece of toast at me (still trying not to smile). "I'll pay him five bucks to rake. If he wants to flirt, that's going to *cost* him five."

"He can flirt for free at Evie's party," teased Ian, getting in on the fun.

Mom rolled her eyes. "Don't remind me. Hannah's first boy-girl party!" She took my father's hand. "We must be getting old, honey."

"Spotless," said Dad to me. "I see one leaf, the kid is banned from this house forever." At that, he finally broke into a grin.

I put on old jeans and a baggy sweatshirt, then pulled my long hair into a ponytail. I thought about using some Luscious Peach on my lips, but decided to go with the natural look. After all, raking leaves is a very natural activity.

I got a rake and a box of trash bags out of the garage, and kicked a few leaves around while I waited for Bruce. There was a breeze, and the sky was the blue of pool water.

Finally, Bruce rounded the corner of the house. "Hi, Hannah."

"Hi, Bruce." I handed him a rake. "How's business?"

"Great! Yours is my third lawn this morning. Yesterday I did four. That's thirty-five bucks!"

"Wow!" The late-morning sun fell in shapeless patches across the leaves. His raking made a crisp rhythm. "Are you saving up for something?"

"Sure am," he told me, not breaking the pattern of swift sweeps. "A mountain bike. If I rake till it snows, then shovel till it melts, then cut grass all spring, I'll have enough money to buy the bike by summer."

"Sounds like a lot of work." I watched him rake for a few minutes. "Can I get you a Coke or anything?" I was hoping he'd say yes, and sit at the patio table with me to drink it, but Bruce was all business.

"Time is money," he said, glancing up with a smile.

"Well, maybe I could help you. We've got another rake."

"Thanks anyway." He paused to adjust his grip. "But I'll make you a deal . . . You can bring me my first Coke tonight at Evie's party." He smiled broadly, and I felt my stomach flip. It was such a cute, flirty thing to say! His eyes were sparkling blue, like the sky.

Instinctively, I tossed my hair. "You got it," I said, and turned to start across the lawn. I was almost to the patio when Bruce called, "This is going to be a party no one will ever forget."

I let his words tumble to the grass like so many autumn leaves. It never occurred to me to panic.

fourteen

I WAS THE FIRST TO ARRIVE at Evie's party. Her gift was wrapped and hidden in my overnight bag. I also had a grocery bag full of last-minute things she'd forgotten to pick up: birthday candles, extra napkins, pretzels, and lemons for the iced tea.

"Happy birthday!" I cried when she opened the door. She noticed right away that I was wearing Luscious Peach lipstick. I noticed that in addition to the usual blush Evie was wearing eyeshadow for the occasion.

"Thanks!" She was holding a partially blown up balloon in her lips. "I'm glad you're early! You can help me decorate!"

We were just taping up the last purple streamer when the doorbell rang.

Evie screamed. I laughed. We hugged. The first boy-girl party was beginning.

Mrs. Neville escorted Ashley Wells, Kimberly, Eddie, and Todd into the enormous family room. They seemed impressed with our decorating efforts. Eddie seemed more impressed with the pool table. Evie beamed.

"Where's the stereo?" asked Todd, and with that became officially responsible for the music for the evening.

When Sheila arrived, the first thing she said was "Where's

Bruce?" Then she looked me over and asked me why I wasn't wearing my new shirt. Her tone made me feel like she thought just about *anything* would look better than what I had on. I avoided both questions and handed her a sugar cookie.

Then the doorbell rang again and I could hear Bruce's voice in the foyer, offering to rake the Nevilles' yard for five dollars. Sheila gave me a phony smile.

I practically sprinted to the kitchen to grab a Coke out of the fridge. It took a minute to decide whether or not to bring him a straw; I chose not to. In the family room, Bruce and Eddie were already racking the balls for a game of pool.

"Your Coke," I said, surprised at how shy I sounded. It was Eddie's shot, and Bruce was leaning on his pool cue.

"Thanks." Bruce opened the can and the metallic pop of it made me jump. He laughed, took a sip, then asked me to hold the can while he took his turn. He sank two balls with one shot. I felt a tingle along my spine like the fizz from the soda. As far as I was concerned, this was the best party I'd ever been to in my life.

In a while, Mr. and Mrs. Neville served pizza. Most of us sat on the floor and ate. Evie gave all the pepperoni from her slice to Dennis because he was a big pepperoni fan (so was Evie!). The boys talked about football and the girls pretended to be interested. Then Alex Delaney suggested we play Spin the Bottle and everyone giggled, but the game never actually got under way.

I could see Evie was just itching to open her presents, so I whispered to Bruce to help me carry them to the center of the room.

"Happy birthday, Evie!" everyone shouted, and she began tearing into her gifts. She made a big fuss over the purse and especially the matching makeup case.

Some of the boys had chipped in and bought her a pair of

ice skates, which was a great gift. Evie was thrilled that Dennis had bought something on his own: a teddy bear with a pink satin bow around its neck.

When the gifts were all open, Evie thanked us, then said it was time for cake. We all went into the kitchen and Bruce asked me for another Coke, which I was happy to get for him.

Just as Evie blew out the candles, the doorbell rang. She looked at me, and I shrugged. Everyone we'd invited was already there.

Then I noticed the boys whispering to one another, laughing and craning their necks to see the kitchen doorway, through which Mr. Neville had just disappeared to answer the door.

"Well, Evie," came her father's voice down the hall. "We've got a late arrival."

And there he was, in the doorway. Malcolm Murgatroyd, wearing a suit and bow tie and holding a very nicely wrapped birthday gift.

"Happy birthday, Evie," he said, smiling.

The boys began to laugh hysterically, and before long, Sheila and the two Ashleys were cracking up, too. Mr. and Mrs. Neville looked totally confused. Evie was on the verge of tears.

I had no idea what I was feeling.

My eyes shot from Malcolm to the boys, then back to Malcolm. He looked different. It took me a second to realize it was his hair. It was clean, full, not in the least bit oily. And he had combed it in a way that made him look, from the forehead up at least, a lot like Dr. Steve. Unfortunately, I was the only one who noticed the improvement in Malcolm's hairstyling technique.

For a moment, he smiled as if he thought he'd just missed a great joke, but soon he realized what the joke was: him.

"Didn't you see the sign on the door, Murganerd?" Dennis said through his laughter. "No losers allowed!"

But Malcolm wasn't looking at Dennis; he was looking at me. He was looking *to* me. I was the one who was supposed to help him; he needed me more than ever. I opened my mouth, but the laughter around me was growing louder. And I knew, if I said anything in Malcolm's defense, they'd be laughing at me.

"Boys!" said Mrs. Neville firmly. "I want you to stop right now. This is very unkind."

I turned to look at Evie; tears were welling up in her eyes. The party was ruined. The boys' laughter quieted to a giggling ripple. Malcolm remained in the kitchen doorway, and I could feel him looking at me. Waiting for me to save him— waiting, maybe, for me to say, "Sit down, Malcolm. Glad you could make it. Have some cake?"

Or perhaps to say, "Shut up, you jerks! Malcolm is my friend. You're hurting him."

But this time I said nothing.

Suddenly Malcolm stepped into the kitchen. The room became uncomfortably quiet. In his annoying, bouncy walk, Malcolm went right up to Evie, who was still poised above the candles. "Happy birthday," he said again. "I'm sorry for the mistake. I received an invitation so . . . I thought you wanted me to come." He put his package very carefully on the table, turned, and ran out the door. Mr. Neville hurried after him, probably to drive him home.

Mrs. Neville's hands were planted firmly on her hips. "I hope you boys are proud of yourselves."

The crummy thing was, they were. Evie's mother cut the cake, then marched out of the room and didn't come back til nine to tell the boys it was time to go. I wished I could go, too. I was not in the mood for a slumber party.

We did the usual slumber-party things: Evie let us use her

makeup, we danced a little, and then we talked about boys. Sheila said she thought it was a great joke for the boys to send Malcolm an invitation. "What a nerd! He actually thought he was invited."

Much, much later, when the others had all fallen asleep in their sleeping bags on Evie's bedroom floor, I reached up and nudged my best friend in her bed.

"You asleep?" I whispered to the darkness.

"No."

"Me, neither." I heard the rustling of sheets, then saw Evie getting out of bed. Quietly, I got up and followed her downstairs to the kitchen. We helped ourselves to some cake and milk, and sat down at the kitchen table, where Malcolm's beautifully wrapped gift lay unopened.

"I wonder what it is," she said.

"Open it."

The crinkling of the paper as she unwrapped the present seemed especially loud in the silence of the sleeping house.

"It's lipstick," she said, surprised. "It's Luscious Peach. How did he know?"

I poked around at my cake with the fork. That's what he'd been buying at Lord and Taylor. He remembered I told him Evie had given me hers, and he'd gone out and bought her a new one. The cake felt like lead in my stomach. I explained to Evie.

"Wow" was all she said at first. "After I've been so rotten to him. Boy, do I feel like a creep."

"What about me?" I asked, too loud in the quiet kitchen. "I'm supposed to look after him. At least, I always do. And tonight I just . . ." I took a sip of milk and paused. "Did you see his bow tie?" I sighed. "He really thought this was something special."

"I wonder what his parents thought when my dad brought him home," said Evie softly.

I could have guessed. The thought of it made my heart hurt. I could just picture Kate, helping with his tie and fixing his hair, and being so happy he was finally invited somewhere. And then I imagined her face when he came home not even twenty minutes later, crying probably. She'd tell him not to feel bad, that he didn't need friends like that, and Dr. Steve would tousle his son's hair and say, "It's okay, kiddo," and when Malcolm was asleep, Kate would lie awake and cry.

I wondered if Kate and Dr. Steve knew I was at the party.

Wasn't it only a few days ago that Malcolm hid under a blanket in my mother's car to keep me from getting laughed at?

In a little while, Evie and I went back to bed, but it was hours before I finally fell asleep.

fifteen

I STAYED AT THE NEVILLES' HOUSE until noon to help Evie and her mom clean up. Actually, I was just stalling. Malcolm had probably called and told Ian everything about last night by now, and Ian had probably told my parents.

Mrs. Neville was dumping pretzel and potato-chip crumbs out of bowls and into a trash bag. Evie and I avoided her eyes as long as we could. Finally, she stopped dumping abruptly and said, "Girls, I think what you did to that poor Malcolm last night was horrible."

"We didn't do it, Mom," said Evie. "The boys did. They invited him behind my back."

"I realize that, Evie, but when Malcolm showed up, you should have been polite." Mrs. Neville shook her head. "Oh, that poor boy."

Evie looked at me. I cleared my throat and tried to sound respectful. "But, Mrs. Neville, you don't understand. If Evie had asked Malcolm to stay, the kids would have laughed at *her*. It would have ruined the party. I know it sounds bad, but that's just how it is!"

Evie nodded fervently. "Right. That's how it is. It's not our fault."

Mrs. Neville frowned. "I thought you two had more guts than that." She handed the trash bag to Evie and left.

We were quiet for a little while, cleaning up the rest of the mess. Then I said, "I guess I should get going."

"Yeah, I guess."

I collected my pajamas and sleeping bag. Then I took Malcolm's coat from the front hall, where he'd left it in his rush to escape. "I'll take this," I told Evie. I didn't have to make up an excuse, since she knew the truth. It was a relief not to have to lie.

Evie walked me to the door and when she opened it she asked thoughtfully, "What do you think my mom meant when she said she thought you and I had more guts? What's guts got to do with it?"

"I guess it takes more guts to get laughed at than it does to laugh."

Evie gave an impatient sigh. "You were right. She doesn't understand."

But I stepped off the Nevilles' porch and headed home knowing deep down in my gutless stomach that Evie and I were wrong; Mrs. Neville understood perfectly.

I opened the door and called, "Hello?"

From the other room, Ian responded, "Jerk!"

"That's enough, Ian," came my mother's voice. "I'll handle this." She appeared from the kitchen and, without even looking at me, started up the stairs. "Hannah, I'd like to see you in my room, please."

I followed her upstairs and dropped my sleeping bag and Malcolm's coat outside my bedroom door, then walked down the hall to my parents' room. My mother shut the door behind me and pointed to the bed.

"Sit."

I sat.

Mom began pacing across the room. I could see her anger building as she walked, searching for the right words to express it. I looked around and my eyes rested on the picture of my parents' wedding party, framed on my father's dresser. Dr. Steve, the best man, in his tuxedo (wearing a bow tie, just like Malcolm) and Kate in her bridesmaid's dress smiled gorgeously, perfectly, at me.

"Mom," I blurted, unable to stand her silence for one more second. "Mom, I'm sorry! But what was I supposed to do?"

She glared at me. Then the door opened and my father, who was never at a loss for words, came in.

"Dad, I'm sorry. I'm sorry if Malcolm's feelings were hurt, but—"

He cut me off. "Are you? Are you sorry, really?"

"Well, yeah."

He shook his head, just like Mrs. Neville. "Yeah? Well, I don't believe you. How do you like that?"

I didn't like it. It hurt. My own dad didn't believe me.

"I'm telling the truth. I feel cruddy about it. You should have seen his face." My voice cracked and I blinked at the wedding photo. "And his bow tie."

"We *did* see his face, Hannah." My mother finally found her voice. "He had Evie's father drop him here." She gave a small, sad laugh. "He told us he left because the party was dull. He said he was bored—no one to talk space aliens with. He told us he asked Mr. Neville to drop him here because he thought he might be able to help Ian with that math that's been troubling him." Mom paused, looking from me to Dad, then back to me. "But we knew that wasn't the truth."

Dad's arms were folded across his chest. "It took a while, but we finally got him to tell us what really happened."

"Did he cry?" I heard myself asking.

"No," said Mom. "But you know something? I wish he had, because it was just awful to see him sitting here, trying to tell the story with his head up, trying so hard to be brave.

He told us he didn't want to go home because he knew Kate and Steve would have felt bad and he wanted to spare their feelings." Mom threw up her arms. "He came here because he was too embarrassed—too *humiliated*, Hannah—to go home and face his parents. He came here because he didn't want them to know what you and your friends did to him." She was crying now. "Good Lord, Hannah, do you have any idea how cruel that was?"

I nodded. My throat was tight. "I know. But I didn't do it. I didn't even know the boys invited him. I didn't know about it until he came in."

"Well, why didn't you do something *then*?" Dad was almost shouting. "You didn't say anything, you didn't stick up for him, you just stood there and let them laugh at him."

"I couldn't. Don't you see? I *couldn't*." I was crying now, too. "They would have laughed at me. They would have laughed at me like they laughed at him."

"And you don't think it would have been worth it?" Dad demanded. "To be laughed at for a friend?"

"He's not my friend, he's my responsibility. Every time he does something dumb or obnoxious, I run to his rescue." I fought back the strangling feeling in my chest. "I try and try to keep Malcolm out of trouble, but he just keeps acting like a creep, and I'm tired of it. I don't want to be laughed at. I don't want people to make fun of me like they do Ian."

It was like having a glass of ice water thrown in my face. I never even knew I felt that way. The pain filled me, the pain and the guilt. "Don't they know how mean that is? And don't they know that I know they laugh at him all the time?" I threw myself facedown on the bed and let the tears come.

"Sweetheart . . ." said Dad gently, sitting down beside me and stroking my hair. "Nobody laughs at Ian."

"Yes they do." My voice was muffled in the comforter.

"Not out loud, but they laugh inside. Every time he bumps into the drinking fountain, or tries to throw a ball at recess. And the time he dropped his lunch tray when he first got the chair. And stupid T.J. He probably laughs his stupid head off every time he beats some dorky third-grader in a race." The feelings came rushing out with the tears; the tears rushed out with the pain. I wasn't even sure the words made sense.

Mom sat down, too. "Oh, honey—"

"You know something? They *should* laugh at me. They should laugh at *me* because I'm a stupid jerk who doesn't even know how to act around my own brother. Because I didn't have the guts to ride the bus with him and because I get a stomachache every time I look at his sneakers!"

My breaths were quick and shallow as I gulped in the air and shuddered it out. My shoulders shook. Mom put her arms around me and whispered, "Just cry, baby. Just cry. It's all right."

"I'm so sorry, Mom. I'm sorry I hurt Malcolm." But I wasn't just crying for Malcolm and Kate and Dr. Steve. I was crying for Ian and me and for my parents and for Jeffrey in special ed and his parents. I was crying for everything. I didn't know it could hurt so much.

"Every time I kick a kickball or run the hurdles in phys ed, I think, Ian will never do this. Ever." I shivered, trying to get a breath. "It's not fair that I can walk and he can't. He keeps getting weaker and weaker and I just keep walking and running . . . Sometimes I feel like I'm hogging all the muscles." It was such a stupid thing to say that for a moment I laughed. I must have seemed like a crazy person. "You know what I mean." Then the laughter was gone and a fresh burst of tears came. "I can't do anything to protect Ian—*anything*—but Ian loves Malcolm, so I try to protect Malcolm. And last night I let him down. And I let Ian down. I'm so, so sorry."

Dad continued to stroke my hair. His hands were rough from the work on Ian's room, but his words were soft, echoing my mom's. "Just cry, baby," he whispered. "Go ahead and cry."

I must have fallen asleep there on the deep, soft comforter of my parents' bed, because when I woke up the room was softly golden with late-afternoon sun. My eyes felt swollen and they stung. I hadn't slept much at Evie's and the whole episode with my parents just knocked me out. I lay still for a moment, watching the autumn sunset glow beyond the leafless trees. Then I rolled over, picked up the phone, and dialed the Murgatroyds's number, hoping Kate or Steve didn't answer.

"Hello?"

"Celeste?"

"Olivia."

"Oh, hi, Liv. It's Hannah." Nothing. I swallowed hard. "Is Malcolm home?"

For a little kid, Olivia had a pretty quick wit. She said, "Of course he's home. Where else would he be, Hannah? At a birthday party?"

I heard her place the receiver down roughly and call for her brother. In a moment, I heard the click of the extension being picked up and Malcolm's voice saying, "Hello?"

"Malcolm, it's me. Hannah. I want to apologize about last night. I should have told them to stop laughing."

"Well, you did what you thought you had to do."

"It was a rotten thing for Bruce and those guys to do and I swear, if I'd known what they were planning, I would have stopped them. I swear. I'm sorry, Malcolm. You didn't deserve that. Oh, and Evie feels bad, too. She really does. And she"—these words caught in my throat—"she loved the lipstick. That was really cool of you, Malcolm."

He let a long moment pass before he said, "Apology accepted."

"Thanks, Malcolm."

"And, Hannah, I've come to a decision. I don't want you to feel like you have come to my rescue from now on. I don't want you to stick up for me or anything like that."

"Why not?"

"Because you did what you had to do. Now I'll have to do what I have to do."

"Oh. All right." Then I remembered. "You left your coat at Evie's. I brought it home. I was going to walk it over. Okay?"

"Whatever."

"Okay. See you in a bit, then."

"See you, Hannah."

I hung up. The sun had vanished behind the trees. Malcolm's coat was still on the floor outside my bedroom door. I snatched it up and called, "Be right back, Mom," and I was down the stairs and out the door before she could reply.

sixteen

I WENT TO THE SIDE DOOR at the Murgatroyds'. Not because I didn't want to be spotted on his doorstep, but because Kate was very particular about her marble foyer, so anyone under the age of twenty was expected to enter through the mud-room off the kitchen. I knocked on the door and smiled weakly when Dr. Steve appeared.

He smiled back, which surprised me a little. "Hello there, Hannah," he said, but it wasn't that Someday-you'll-be-my-daughter-in-law voice he usually used.

"Hi." I stepped in cautiously, half expecting Celeste and Olivia to ambush me from the breakfast nook. I held out Malcolm's coat. "I took this home from . . . uh, I mean, Malcolm forgot . . ."

"Thanks." Dr. Steve took the coat and hung it on one of the mudroom's many hooks. I looked at him; if he weren't a doctor, he could have been a movie star, he was so handsome. I wondered what Sheila McElroy and the Ashleys would have done if Dr. Steve had walked into Evie's party unannounced. Fainted, probably. "Hannah, have you got a minute?"

I nodded.

"Good. I'd like to talk to you." He put his hand on my shoulder and led me through the kitchen and across the enormous living room to his study. In all the years I'd been coming to the Murgatroyds' house, I'd never seen the inside of Dr. Steve's study. It was off-limits to kids, even his kids. He asked me to have a seat in a huge leather chair and slid himself up onto the edge of his desk and sat there, casually swinging his feet. He was so cool. He was so incredibly cool; suddenly I was mad at him for it. He was still smiling, but I felt my jaw set.

"Malcolm didn't want to tell us what happened at the party," he began.

But I was so mad at Dr. Steve I was hardly listening. He had to have known all along what a complete washout Malcolm was as a kid, how totally non-athletic he was, that his hair was greasy and his sneakers were outdated and his clothes were a joke. And those *glasses*! This man was a medical professional, for goodness' sake—hadn't he ever heard of contact lenses?

"He told us he left early because he had to help Ian with homework—same thing he told your folks. Finally, though, he told us what really went on."

He was quiet for a while and I was afraid to open my mouth for fear of screaming at him. He was smart and good-looking; he had no idea what Malcolm's life was like. Dr. Steve picked up a football that had been sitting on the desk and began tossing it up and catching it. "When Malcolm was seven, I took him out in the back yard to have a catch." Dr. Steve kept tossing and laughed gently, almost to himself. "He caught the ball twice; we were out there for an hour and a half."

Now he was picking on his own kid! I couldn't believe it.

"But he had heart, I've got to give him that. He didn't quit, he didn't give up . . ."

"Did he cry?" I asked.

"No."

"Oh. Because he usually cries." Before he could go on with his story, I spoke. "Dr. Steve, I'm really sorry that Malcolm was hurt last night. I know I should have told the kids to shut up but, well, to be honest, I didn't have the guts. But you know something?" I decided that my sitting here in his private study meant I could talk to him straight. "Sometimes it seems like Malcolm sets himself up for this kind of stuff. I mean, he could have come to me with the invitation and asked if Evie *really* invited him. He knows those guys, he knows they like to play those mean jokes on him. He must have at least suspected it."

Dr. Steve just nodded.

"He brought Cecil to school the other day, did you know that?"

He shook his head. "I didn't know that."

I glanced around the room, the framed diplomas, the shelves of football trophies and baseball trophies and pictures of Dr. Steve in his various college uniforms. "I guess it's hard for you to understand," I said. I couldn't help the slightly sarcastic tone in my voice.

He spun the football in his hands. "Why do you say that, Hannah?"

"Because." I tried to think of how my mother would put it, politely. "Because you never went through an awkward stage, like Malcolm. He's going to be a late bloomer."

At this, my father's best friend laughed out loud. "Is that what you think?" he said, grinning broadly, his beautiful brown eyes crinkling at the corners. "Didn't your old man ever tell you how we met?"

"No." I couldn't imagine how that would have anything to do with Malcolm being such a geek.

Dr. Steve pushed himself gracefully off the desk, still laughing, and went to one of the many bookshelves. "Well, then. *I'll* tell you." He ran his finger along a row of gilt-printed spines, his yearbooks. He stopped at one and slipped it out of its place, then flipped through the pages until he found what he was looking for. He squatted down beside me and laid the book in my lap. "Recognize anybody?" I didn't. He pointed to a picture. "C'mon. Use your imagination."

The boy in the picture was about fifteen and as scrawny as anyone I'd ever seen. His nose was too big for his face, his ears were too big for his head, and he had the neck of an ostrich.

My mouth fell open. "Don't even tell me—"

"Yep." He nodded. "That's me, sophomore year of high school."

I stared at the picture. Printed beneath it was STEVEN W. MURGATROYD, along with NATIONAL HONOR SOCIETY, SCIENCE CLUB, LATIN CLUB PRESIDENT. I was stunned.

All I could think of to say was "President of the Latin Club, huh?"

Dr. Steve stood and leaned against his desk. "Your dad saved me from getting my head bashed in by some big kid who wanted my math homework."

"Really?"

"Really. That's how we met. He sort of took me under his wing after that. That summer, he got me started on weight training, taught me to throw a fifty-yard pass, and introduced me to his next-door neighbor, this beautiful blonde named Kate."

I couldn't take my eyes off the picture. "So you were a late bloomer?"

"You could say that."

"So can't you speed up Malcolm's blooming a little? Get him a weight set or something?"

Dr. Steve shrugged. "I suppose I could." He smiled. "I know the kids give Malcolm a hard time, and Kate and I hate to see him hurt. But there are so many good things about Malcolm, things that are a lot more important than throwing a football." He smiled. "We just stay focused on those things. We try not to let things like Evie's party get to us." For a moment, we were quiet. Then he said, "It's dark. I'll drive you home."

It was only a couple of blocks from the Murgatroyds' house to my house. I kept picturing Dr. Steve, before and after. Malcolm was definitely still in his "before" period. I pictured Malcolm sitting down with my parents and trying to be brave, not telling them what happened.

When I got out of the car, I held the door open for a second and said, "Dr. Steve, I know Malcolm can't throw a football or anything like that, but you know what? He's got more guts than Bruce Wyatt and Dennis Duffy put together."

Dr. Steve didn't know Bruce Wyatt or Dennis Duffy, but I think he knew exactly what I meant. He grinned. "Thank you, Hannah. See you at the wedding."

For the first time ever, I considered the possibility.

seventeen

ON MONDAY, several significant events took place: Malcolm Murgatroyd was absent for the first time in his entire academic career, Bruce Wyatt held my hand behind the gym annex at recess, and my little brother was rushed to the hospital to fight for his life.

When I dragged myself into the classroom on Monday morning, the boys were in their usual corner, congratulating themselves on what they'd done to Malcolm.

Bruce spotted me right away. "Hey, Hannah, great party! You think Murgaturd enjoyed himself?" The other boys laughed and Bruce smiled at me. The smile wasn't for the joke on Malcolm, though; the smile was for me bringing him Cokes and because we'd sat next to teach other while Evie opened her gifts. Any other day, that smile would have made my knees wobble. Today it made me queasy.

They went on gloating over their cleverness. I tried not to listen. Instead, I plunked myself down at my desk and went over my autobiography, which was due that day. I skimmed the section about the day I took the training wheels off my bike; Malcolm had been there. I reread the part about our big adventure at the shore, the year there was a hurricane; Malcolm had taped up the windows with my father. Then I checked over the three pages about how we found out about Ian's disease. In that section, every other word should have been "Malcolm," but the fact was, his name did not appear once, not there or anywhere else in my entire paper. Not with the training wheels, not during the hurricane, not ever. In other words, I'd completely written Malcolm Murgatroyd out of my life. I think there's an expression: *The pen is mightier than the sword.* Now I knew what it meant.

It wasn't until Miss Lindstrum took attendance that I noticed Malcolm was absent. The teacher was as surprised as I was and even went to the door to look for him in the hall. This year, like every year, Malcolm was shooting for the Perfect Attendance record. Suddenly, I wanted him to get the award as badly as if it were an Olympic gold medal. I held my breath, hoping he'd been detained on some important hall-monitor business, like maybe a fifth-grader had been running in the corridor. Miss Lindstrum seemed to be hoping the same thing. Finally, she closed the door and marked Malcolm absent. Then she told us to pass our autobiographies to the front.

After we handed in our papers, Miss Lindstrum said, "Take out your social-studies books, people."

This was followed by the rustle of papers, the hollow clunks of hardcovers hitting desktops, and the teacher saying, "You'll have to look on with your neighbor," when Dennis Duffy raised his hand and told her he couldn't find his social-studies book. It was ordinary, daily, normal stuff. And Malcolm was missing it.

Miss Lindstrum assigned pages in the textbook and gave us thirty minutes for silent reading. About halfway through, Miss Jacobs, the vice principal, came in with a manila envelope. I heard her whisper to Miss Lindstrum that Dr. Murgatroyd had dropped it off in the main office. It was Malcolm's autobiography. Vaguely, I wondered why Kate hadn't been the one to bring it, but then I remembered that Monday was Dr. Steve's day off from the hospital. I watched as the teacher placed the envelope carefully on top of the pile of autobiographies at the corner of her desk and my stomach flipped. I couldn't get it out of my mind that Malcolm had messed up his shot at the Perfect Attendance award which he'd been bragging about since the third grade—and it was our fault.

Part of the chapter in our social-studies book was about people in the olden days arranging marriages. That certainly hit home! The book explained that young women were promised by their parents to young men, and these women had to have something called a dowry, like cows or land or money, to get these men to marry them. Most of the time, the young men and women didn't even meet until the day they got married.

After a half hour, Miss Lindstrum looked around the room. "Who would like to comment on the reading?"

I wriggled in my seat, debating whether or not to raise my hand, since I did have personal experience with this sort of thing. Then I heard Miss Lindstrum say, "Yes, Bruce."

Everyone turned to look at him. He was the last person I'd expect to want to comment on anything as girlish as marriage, arranged or otherwise.

"Well," he said, shrugging, "I just think it would be really, ya know, crummy to make your kid get married to somebody they didn't, ya know, love."

Gentle laughter rippled through the room and Miss Lindstrum said, "People . . ." She nodded at Bruce to continue. I noticed that Sheila was looking at him with big, dopey eyes and a weird, dreamy smile.

Bruce cleared his throat and went on. "You shouldn't make a person marry somebody just 'cause you need a few cows or whatever. It's just dumb."

Miss Lindstrum leaned against her desk and smiled. "Okay. That's a good point. But let's look at this from a more contemporary point of view." She put down her book and tapped her chin. "Let's say, Bruce, that your dad owns an ice-cream parlor—the only ice-cream parlor for miles around. And let's say that everyone in town comes there for ice cream and your most popular item is your famous double-chocolate sundae with whipped cream and rainbow shots."

Bruce grinned. "With a cherry on top?"

"Yes!" said Miss Lindstrum. "Yes, with a cherry on top. As a matter of fact, that cherry happens to be the single most important component of the sundae, because your father uses only the most delicious, delectable cherries available, which he purchases at a bulk discount from the nearby Billings Cherry Orchard, which, by coincidence, is owned and operated by Hannah's father. Now, Hannah works at the orchard part-time on weekends, and sometimes, Bruce, you go along with your dad when he goes to pick up his weekly order of cherries."

I felt myself blushing, in spite of the horrible mood I was in. A few kids, like Dennis Duffy and Alex Delaney, went "Oooohhh," but Miss Lindstrum ignored them. Sheila seemed to be sulking.

"Hannah," said the teacher, pointing at me, "you work the produce scale at the orchard and you've met Bruce on a couple of occasions, but that's the extent of your relationship, since you have your sights set on a certain young man who works in the pickle factory across town." Everybody cracked up at that. I could feel Bruce looking at me, and I laughed, too.

"Then, Bruce, guess what happens!"

"What?"

"Someone opens up *another* ice-cream parlor right down the street from your dad's. And their specialty is a *triple-*

chocolate sundae with whipped cream and rainbow sprinkles."

The class started booing and Bruce pretended to be very, very angry. Miss Lindstrum started walking around the classroom as she talked. "The only thing that's keeping your dad in business are those delicious, delectable cherries from Billings Orchard, because, for the moment anyway, the owner of the new ice-cream parlor hasn't cultivated a business relationship with Mr. Billings."

"Hey," Dennis blurted without raising his hand. "I get it. If Bruce marries Hannah, then Hannah's dad won't sell cherries to the new guy, because Bruce will be his son-in-law."

"Exactly!" said Miss Lindstrum. "And now you understand why people would arrange marriages. What the practice lacks in romance, it makes up for in profit."

Some kids applauded. It was one of the better social-studies lessons we'd had so far, and we were all a little disappointed to have to put away our social-studies texts and take out our math folders, since Miss Lindstrum rarely got that creative with long division. Still, it lightened me up a little, and when Bruce passed my desk on his way to sharpen a pencil, he gave me a very flirty look, like the whole sundae story had actually been true. I had half a mind to go home and talk my father into giving up his career as an architect and taking up cherry farming. After all, a cherry farmer would never have any reason to marry his daughter off to the nerdy son of a renowned surgeon.

eighteen

By LUNCHTIME, the lightheartedness I'd been feeling over the social-studies lesson had begun to wear off and my guilt about Malcolm was returning. On top of that, outdoor recess was canceled because of the cold. An early November chill had set in, sparkling with frost and promising a harsh and sudden winter. The principal opened the auxiliary gymnasium for indoor recess and we were told to go there, instead of outside to the playground, directly from lunch.

Evie crumpled up her lunch bag and dropped it into the garbage can. "There's nothing to do during indoor recess." She wrinkled her nose. "It's no fun. It's dull."

The auxiliary gym was loud and crawling with fifth- and sixth-graders. Evie and I spotted the Ashleys sitting on the balance beam. They waved us over, giggling.

"Guess what!" Ashley Perillo was about ready to explode. "Guess what Bruce told Dennis, who told Alex, who told me!"

Evie took the bait; I didn't really care. "Okay, Ashley," said Evie, "*what* did Bruce tell Dennis, blah, blah, blah?"

That was when Sheila appeared and said, "What's going on?"

"Bruce wants to talk to Hannah outside behind the annex!"

The Ashleys practically shrieked. Evie's mouth dropped open.

Sheila rolled her eyes. "I'll believe it when I see it," she muttered.

I felt my face turn pink and once again the sinking feeling in my stomach began to disappear. "Really?"

Ashley Wells nodded. "Really!"

"Talking behind the annex" was actually a code that the sixth-graders passed down year after year, and it meant that Bruce was going to ask me to be his girlfriend. The routine was to sneak out behind the auxiliary gym during recess, then the boy asks you out, then you scrape your initials into the brick wall of the annex and it's official.

Evie threw her arms around me and gave me a hug. "And I thought this was going to be *dull*! Hannah, couldn't you just die?"

The darkness lifted; I wasn't thinking about Malcolm or the birthday party or anything except going outside with Bruce. All I could think of to say was "Oh, my gosh."

The annex doors were open, framing the bright, cold afternoon for us, and letting a welcome gust of cool into the crowded gym.

"Hannah!" Evie grabbed both my hands. "Are you going to?"

Out of the corner of my eye, I could see Bruce tossing a basketball up in the air and catching it, sort of the way Dr. Steve had done in his study. For a second, I wondered what Bruce's dad was like. Then he saw me—I think he must have been nervous, because he missed the ball. I waved. He waved. Then Dennis Duffy gave him a shove and Bruce was on his way over to the balance beam.

"Hi, Hannah.'

"Hi, Bruce." He was looking at me as if Evie, Sheila, and the Ashleys weren't even there. "What's up?"

He shrugged, sort of shifting his weight. "Cold out, huh?"

I glanced at Evie. Her eyes were wide and she was shaking her head fast. "Well," I answered, "no, it's not *too* cold. Not really."

He seemed relieved. "Yeah, that's what I was thinking. It's not too cold."

Sheila nudged Ashley Perillo and asked in a sly voice, "Not too cold for *what*?"

Bruce jammed his hands into his pockets. "Not too cold for a walk. Or something."

Sheila whispered, "Or *something*," and rolled her eyes. Across the gym I could see the Alexes watching us; Dennis had vanished.

"So, Hannah. Feel like goin' for a walk?"

"Okay. Sure."

Mr. Donaldson, the gym teacher, was recess monitor and he happened to be busy untangling the climbing ropes that some stupid fifth-grader had managed to knot up. Bruce made his escape through the open door and I darted out behind him.

It was like diving into a cold pool on a hot day, bursting into the chilly sunlight from the stuffy gym. My cheeks tingled and I felt light, as if I might rise up off the ground and get stuck in a leafless tree. The first thing Bruce said was "Are you cold?"

"No. It feels good."

He shivered. "Yeah. It feels good." But I could tell he was freezing. "That was pretty funny, all that ice-cream stuff, huh?"

I laughed, nodding. "To tell the truth, I was sort of surprised that you, well, ya know, felt that way about it."

"About ice-cream sundaes?"

"No, about, um, love."

"Oh." He cupped his hands to his mouth and blew on

them. "Oh, that." He shrugged. "I just can't see somebody's parents forcing them to get married to a person. Like, what if your parents picked somebody gross?" His eyes lit up with laughter and he smiled. "Like, what if your parents wanted to marry you off to a creep like Murgatroyd?" He laughed out loud.

A gust of icy wind hit me in the back. "What's that supposed to mean?"

He kept chuckling. "Man, that would stink, wouldn't it? Your parents selling you out to a geek like Murgatroyd." He found this hilarious. I found it terrifying. Had he found out somehow?

"Why would you say that?" I demanded. "I mean, why would you even think of me and Malcolm getting married?"

Bruce looked confused. "No reason. He's just the geekiest guy I could think of."

"Oh." I exhaled, relieved. My breath made a small cloud between us. "Well, we didn't come out here to talk about Malcolm, did we?" It was a pretty bold thing to say, but I wanted to get off the subject of my engagement.

"No." Bruce took a few steps toward me, confident, like the day he raked leaves in my yard. "I wanted to ask you something."

I folded my arms across my chest for warmth. "Yes?"

He was so cute, standing there in the cold with his cheeks all red and the sun shining in his hair. He rubbed his hands together, then reached out and took my hand in his. "Wanna be my girlfriend? I mean, would you go out with me?"

My heart was pounding so fast I wondered if he could hear it. "Great. I mean, yeah."

"Yeah?"

I nodded. "Uh-huh."

"Cool." He blinked into the bright sunlight and loosened

his grip on my hand. For a second, I thought he was going to let go; instead, he arranged his fingers between mine and closed them again so they were all woven together, snug and warm. "Very cool."

Then he found a small sharp stone and began scraping our initials into the brick, next to the initials and hearts and arrows that had been left there by years and years of sixth-graders. He carved with one hand and held mine with the other.

"Hey," he said suddenly, finishing up the "W." "We're the first ones in our class to come out here and . . . you know."

It was exhilarating. "Wow. You're right."

Before I could say anything else, though, Dennis Duffy stuck his head out the door and called, "Wyatt! Get in here! You're not going to believe this!"

Bruce didn't let go of my hand until we stepped inside. He seemed a little angry at Dennis for interrupting us. I was furious. Dennis and the boys were waiting in the doorway with Evie, Sheila, and the Ashleys. I hoped Sheila noticed that Bruce had been holding my hand.

"Okay, Duffy," Bruce snapped. "So what's so important?"

From behind his back, Dennis produced a manila envelope. He had a wicked smile on his face. "I snagged Murgadork's autobiography from Lindstrum's desk."

"You did *what*?" said Bruce and I together.

Dennis rolled his eyes. "Isn't that cute? They're so in love they've only got one voice!"

Bruce shook his head. "You're gonna get killed for that when Lindstrum finds out."

My throat was dry and my heart was pounding even faster than it had been when Bruce took my hand. "Why? Why would you steal his homework?"

Dennis shook the envelope in my face. "Don't you ever

wonder what his pathetic life is like? I bet it's all about how he collects butterflies, or reads the dictionary for fun. Maybe there's even pictures!"

Pictures! The Murgatroyds' pictures were as full of us as ours were of them. Dennis began opening the envelope and my knees almost buckled. I practically shouted, "Don't!"

Dennis sneered at me. "Hey, Wyatt, tell your girlfriend not to be such a Goody Two-shoes, will ya? Everybody wants to see ol' Nerd Boy hanging around the chessboard with his Nerd Family." He turned to the others. "Right, guys?" Everyone nodded. Dennis tore open the envelope and removed Malcolm's perfectly typed paper. I was afraid I was going to be sick. Evie was wringing her hands.

Dennis cleared his throat as if he was about to read us the Declaration of Independence. Imitating Malcolm's screechy voice, he read: "I am Malcolm Steven Murgatroyd and I am eleven and a half years old. I have two sisters, Celeste and Olivia, and they are twins. My father is a surgeon. He is chief of staff at St. Vincent's Hospital."

"His father's a surgeon?" said Sheila.

My head was spinning. Dennis read on. "Before she married my father, my mother was a dancer with the City Ballet Company." Dennis studied the snapshot that was paperclipped to the page. "Man. These people can't be related to Murgatroyd." He held up the picture.

The Ashleys looked at Dr. Steve and their eyes almost popped out of their heads. The same went for the boys, gawking at Kate and her long, shining hair and perfect figure.

"Those aren't his parents," Sheila said. "He must have cut that out of a magazine or something."

I knew if I made eye contact with Evie I'd burst into tears on the spot. I looked down at the gym floor and stood there, frozen.

Dennis flipped through the pages. "He's gonna get a ton of extra credit on this; look at all the pictures he put . . ." He stopped dead, staring at the last page of the paper. "Holy cow!"

"Now what?" said Bruce. I kept my head low, but raised my eyes enough to see Dennis's face. He looked wicked.

"Ol' Malcolm sure didn't get these from a magazine!" he said, waving a whole page of photos under my nose. "Did he, Hannah?"

I swallowed hard. I had no words. Dennis was loving every minute of it.

He tore one of the pictures off the page and held it up. "Look, guys. Here's little Hannah Billings on her first two-wheeler. And, hey, who's that with her? Why, it's her little friend, Malcolm Murgatroyd."

The tears came, hot and fast down my cheeks.

The Alexes, the Ashleys, and Sheila couldn't make up their minds whether to stare at the pictures or at me. Evie tried to grab the pictures away from Dennis, but he held them above her head. "Cut it out, Dennis," she hissed, but he didn't.

I felt Bruce looking at me but didn't meet his gaze. He took a step away from me, then another. Sheila took a step closer to him. Then another.

Dennis displayed another snapshot. "And here we have Hannah Billings on vacation at the beach with Malcolm. And isn't it just adorable how he's got his scrawny little arm around her? What a cute couple. Hey, Hannah, nice *bathing suit!* Did Murganerd like it?" Everyone cracked up. Dennis passed the picture to Bruce. "Poor Malcolm. Looks like he's got a pretty nasty sunburn there. Hey, Hannah, did you kiss it and make it all better?"

Sheila doubled over at that remark and Dennis made kissy sounds.

Finally, I looked at Bruce. I was desperate. I wanted his help. I needed it. My eyes said, Please make them stop. If you care about me, make them stop hurting me. It was a look he would have recognized if he'd seen Malcolm looking at me the night of Evie's party.

But Bruce did the same thing I did when he saw the look. He did nothing.

So while Dennis and the Alexes and Sheila and the Ashleys were cracking up, I reached out and snatched the autobiography out of Dennis Duffy's grip.

And I ran.

nineteen

EVERYTHING HAPPENS FOR A REASON.

I've heard that: Everything happens for a reason. I heard it over and over again that long-ago summer we found out Ian had muscular dystrophy. It's one of those things people say when they don't know what to say, but, of course, nobody ever could come up with a good reason why a sweet little kid like Ian would be diagnosed with such a horrible, ugly condition and why nice people like my parents and me would have to watch it happen to someone we love. But everything happens for a reason, even Dennis Duffy swiping Malcolm's homework.

And the reason, I suppose, was to get me out of that gym and running into the hall, fast—into the hall, where I saw my mother and father with their coats on, running in from the lobby with the vice principal, Miss Jacobs, and the school nurse and Miss Spalding and Mrs. Bellacristo all standing helplessly out of the way of the paramedics who were putting my brother on a stretcher.

Malcolm's autobiography was in my hand; then, suddenly, it was too heavy to hold. It fell to the floor and the snapshots scattered across the corridor. *Everything happens for a reason.*

Ian was choking. Or gasping. He was crying for Mom to help him. But she couldn't.

They didn't see me. I took a step toward them, but they seemed millions of miles away; I couldn't reach them, I couldn't get there.

Ian kept gasping for breath.

I called out, "Mom! Dad?" but they didn't hear me. Or maybe no sound had come out. I called again. "Mom! *Daddy!*" I was shaking, cold and hot at the same time. Oh God, what was happening to Ian? What was happening to us?

Miss Jacobs turned toward me, her eyes full of tears. She put her hand on my mother's shoulder and whispered something to her which made Mom turn. When she saw me, she opened her arms and that was all it took—I moved forward, as if some unseen hands were gently pushing me toward my family. Then I was in my mother's arms and the paramedics lifted my brother up and carried him through the corridor. Dad followed right behind them, but Mom and I stayed where we were, perfectly still. I think she was thinking what I was thinking: that if we didn't move, if we remained right where we were, nothing else could move either—time would stop and Ian would not get any worse. He wouldn't get put in the ambulance, or taken to the hospital, or stuck full of tubes and needles and hoses.

But then what *would* happen? Would he stay on that stretcher, strapped there, choking for air, gasping for another breath, forever? The thought scared me into motion. I let go of my mother and took off down the hall after Ian and Dad. Mom came running behind me.

Ahead of us, the paramedics were running and Miss Jacobs was running.

Dad was running, too. We were all running.

We were running for Ian's life.

Dr. Steve's Mercedes pulled up to the curb and Kate came flying out of the passenger door practically before the car stopped. Malcolm stayed put in the backseat. Dr. Steve jumped out and went directly to the paramedics, who were putting Ian into the ambulance. Dr. Steve talked fast, with authority, in big words I didn't understand. Then he came over and put his arms around my dad for a moment, before helping him into the ambulance to ride with Ian. Kate was hugging my mother; the two of them were sort of rocking back and forth, rocking each other. I had the silly, unbelievable thought that it looked like they were dancing. Then, without a word, Dr. Steve gently took my mother's arm and assisted her into the ambulance beside my dad.

I don't remember anyone saying anything, making any plans, asking any questions. It was as if they'd been silently, invisibly rehearsing this episode for years. Dr. Steve didn't have to say he would meet them at the hospital; he didn't need to tell them that he'd called ahead and told the ER people to expect us and that he'd personally notified Ian's doctor, who happened to be a golf buddy of his. It was as if it had all been mapped out, arranged in advance. He didn't have to say, "Don't worry, we'll take Hannah with us," because I was already opening the rear door of the Mercedes and getting in.

I guess I'd been planning for this moment, too.

For the first few miles I stayed huddled close to the door, leaving a broad canyon of leather upholstery between Malcolm and myself. Not because I was afraid to be seen in the school driveway sitting beside him—but because I was dizzy and nauseous and thought it might be smart to stay close to the window. And also because, for those first few miles, I was completely frozen with terror and simply could not move.

But the minute I could move, I did. I proceeded as the grownups had, without a word. Silently, I slid across the soft leather car seat toward Malcolm, who reached over and put his arm around me, and I let my head fall onto his shoulder. I did not notice if his hair was oily or not, or if he was clicking his tongue on his teeth. Or if I noticed, I didn't care.

In the front seat, Kate was strumming her long, perfect nails on the armrest and Dr. Steve, whose face I could see in the rearview mirror, was concentrating on the road ahead.

I was lost in my thoughts. Malcolm was saying something —actually, he was singing something, softly.

"Remember that song?' he asked me. His voice sounded the same way it always did, a little screechy and too high-pitched. But it was also familiar and concerned. It was Malcolm. "Remember?" he asked again.

I still couldn't speak. I nodded. I did remember. It was that song from the shore, from the summer I'd had such awful nightmares, right after we learned that Ian was sick. The dreams had been terrifying, all dark and full of Ian suffering and Mom and Dad crying and me helpless through it all. I shuddered; now the dreams were coming true.

What was strange was that I'd put a whole page in my autobiography about the bad dreams but somehow I'd forgotten the words to the song, until now. Malcolm was giving them back to me.

"Ian and I would hear you crying in your sleep," Malcolm said. "And then we'd hear you hollering." Malcolm and Ian always shared a bedroom at the shore, the room with the bunk beds, the one next door to mine, but I hadn't known until now that I'd been waking them up. I felt guilty and cowardly. Ian was the one who should have had the nightmares.

"You sounded really scared," Malcolm was whispering.

"But Mom and Kate would come," I whispered back, finding my voice. "They would come into my room and my mom would hold me and rock me and your mom would sing . . ."

"I remember," said Malcolm. "Ian and I always sang with her. We sang until you went back to sleep." He paused. "Ian really liked that song."

I closed my eyes and looked for the memory, searched for the music, and found it somewhere deep inside, somewhere warm and far away. Then I heard myself singing quietly, "You are my sunshine, my only sunshine . . ."

". . . You make me happy," sang Malcolm, "when skies are gray . . ."

The Mercedes slowed as we turned into the hospital driveway, and I sang into Malcolm's shoulder.

". . . You'll never know, dear, how much I love you . . ."

Dr. Steve parked the car in a reserved spot near the Emergency entrance.

"Please don't take my sunshine . . ."

". . . away."

The sobs came up, hard and fast, from deep inside my chest. Malcolm's arm was around me, holding me, and Kate had climbed into the backseat so she could hold me, too. But Dr. Steve had turned off the engine and it was time to let go.

twenty

LATER—MUCH, MUCH LATER—Evie told me what had happened in the auxiliary gym after I ran out.

Sheila said something about me being the biggest liar in the whole entire world and that nobody should ever talk to me again, not only because I was a complete and total fake but because I actually associated with Malcolm Murgatroyd.

Dennis laughed and said, "Associated? That's an understatement!"

Bruce had sort of turned away from everybody and had his hands stuffed deep into his pockets. "At first," Evie reflected, "I thought he was just embarrassed, ya know? But then I got the feeling he was sort of hurt."

Evie told me that she told Dennis he was the biggest jerk she ever met and that she regretted giving him all the pepperoni off her pizza at the party.

And that's when they heard me yelling for my mom. Everyone ran for the door because—and this part was hard for Evie to admit—the first thing they'd thought was that I'd gone off the deep end over getting caught knowing Malcolm. But then they saw the paramedics and my parents, and Ian strapped down on the stretcher, and they knew it had nothing to do with Malcolm or his autobiography.

I also found out how everybody—my parents and the Murgatroyds—managed to get to school so quickly. As it turned out, Miss Spalding really had come a long way since the day she insisted Malcolm play kickball with us in the third grade. Ian had been helping out in special ed during recess. She got to the phone the minute he showed signs of respiratory failure. First she called the EMS, then she called my mom. Dad was home, too; he had been finishing up the moldings on Ian's bookshelves at the exact same moment that Ian's bronchial tubes gave in, which also happened to be the exact same moment that Dennis Duffy was revealing my secret life to the whole sixth grade. The joke was on Dennis, though—because it was also the exact same moment that I stopped caring about my secret life being a secret.

The really incredible thing was that Ian only had a cold. That was it, a cold. It was dangerous for Ian to get colds now that his muscles were so weak. My little brother was going to be in danger every single day from now on, that was how Dr. Benedict explained it.

Malcolm and I had been sitting in the dimly lit hospital waiting room for hours. Kate looked in on us every half hour or so, but she had no answers, and we didn't know what questions to ask, anyway. Finally, Dr. Benedict, Ian's doctor, arrived and sat down on the low, square end table next to my chair. I must have fallen asleep; he nudged me and I jumped. Malcolm's hand was on top of mine; he jumped, too.

"How's Ian?" I asked.

"He's doing much, much better," the doctor told us. His eyes were kind. "He's going to stay here for a few days and we'll give him medicine, and when his cold is gone, we'll send him home."

Malcolm turned to me and clarified, "They'll give him

antibiotics, so the cold doesn't turn into pneumonia. His lungs aren't strong enough to handle pneumonia."

The doctor's eyebrows shot up and he smiled. "That's exactly right," he said to Malcolm. "I'm impressed."

Malcolm sat tall in his chair and gave the doctor a stuffy look. "I've been researching muscular dystrophy since I was eight. I'm an expert." So, all those hours Malcolm could have spent learning to throw a spiral pass, he'd used to read up on MD, instead. "Ian's my best friend," he told the doctor.

Dr. Benedict nodded. I felt worthless. I was Ian's sister and I didn't know anything. The only thing I could say was "What time is it?"

Kate appeared over the doctor's shoulder and answered, "Ten-thirty. We're going to be leaving soon." She paused and gave us a shaky smile. "Would you like to see Ian before we go?"

Malcolm was on his feet in a flash; my own body seemed to be in slow motion. "Yes," we said together.

Ian was in a private room, not like the hospital rooms on TV sitcoms, where there's always a grumpy old man in the next bed, pulling the curtain closed. My mother was sitting in a hard plastic chair, as close to Ian's face as possible, and Dad was leaning on the foot of the bed, with his head down. Neither of them moved when Malcolm and I stepped in. Dr. Steve put his finger to his lips quickly, in case either one of us was going to say anything, which neither one of us was.

As soon as I saw Ian, I began to cry. He was sleeping, perfectly still except for his labored breathing. He was making terrible noises, gurgling, hissing, rasping. There was a tube stuck in his nose and another stuck into his hand with a needle. He looked pale against the white sheets of the bed, and small, much smaller than he had just this morning when I'd yelled at him for taking the last Ring-Ding for his lunch. He'd stuck his tongue out at me, then sniffled and wiped his nose on his sleeve.

I cried quietly, letting the tears fall from my cheeks and not bothering to wipe them. I hung back, but Malcolm walked right up to Ian and took his hand. I shuffled across the room until I was beside Malcolm.

"He'll be okay," Malcolm whispered.

I nodded hard. Then I hugged my mom and dad and followed Malcolm out of the room. Dr. Steve came out seconds later and led us to the waiting room, where we found Kate and left. Malcolm held the door to the Mercedes open for me and again I slid in across the seat. I remember squeezing my eyes shut and leaning back into the soft leather.

The next thing I knew, I was snuggling into bed in the Murgatroyds' guest room with Cecil the seal tucked carefully under my arm.

twenty-one

"SLEEP OKAY?" MALCOLM was buttering toast in Kate's big, bright kitchen when I came in. Celeste was finishing up her waffles and Olivia was searching for something in the fridge.

"Yeah," I answered. "I guess."

Celeste looked at me anxiously. "Are you scared?"

"Yes."

"Poor Ian," said Olivia, arriving at the table with a pitcher of orange juice.

Malcolm handed me the toast and I took it, realizing I hadn't eaten since lunch yesterday. I glanced up at the clock: 10:15. Naturally, we wouldn't be going to school today. The thought came like a fuzzy daydream. School was in some other dimension that didn't seem to matter.

"Have you heard anything?" I asked, nibbling the toast.

Malcolm motioned toward his father's study. "They're on the phone with your dad now," he said.

I looked at the closed door. Was it really only two days ago that I was talking to Dr. Steve about Malcolm trying to fit in? It seemed so important at the time. Now it was just another blurry thought somewhere in the back of my mind.

Celeste and Olivia finished their breakfast and excused themselves.

I finished the toast and two cups of hot chocolate while I waited for Dr. Steve and Kate to emerge with news. Somewhere in the middle of my second cup, Malcolm cleared his throat and said, "Hannah?"

"Yes?"

"Do you think I'm a coward for not showing up yesterday for school?"

School again, that place from another dimension. School, where kids are cruel and mean and sneaky, where they teach you everything but the important stuff, such as how antibiotics battle pneumonia, or how to look a kid in the eye when you talk about her brother who's in a wheelchair.

"No. I think you're the bravest person I know." And I meant it.

For a moment, we both looked at the closed door and said nothing.

"I wasn't afraid of facing Bruce and those other creeps," said Malcolm, fiddling with the handle of his mug. "I didn't want to face you."

"I don't blame you," I whispered, thinking I understood.

But Malcolm shook his head and said, "Listen. The birthday party was over and done with. I've been the object of Bruce's jokes before, you know. That wasn't the reason I stayed home."

I shrugged. "So what was the reason?"

"I broke my promise."

"What promise?"

"The one we made about never, ever telling that our families are friends." He took a long, deep breath, as if he was about to confess to a terrible crime. "My original autobiography upheld the agreement. I didn't mention you or Ian or your parents once. There were no pictures, nothing." He paused for a sip of cocoa. "But after Evie's party I rewrote the whole thing. And I included several photos of you and me throughout the years."

That's when I realized that Malcolm didn't know yet about Dennis snatching the autobiography and revealing our secret to Bruce and Sheila and the others. But Malcolm looked so utterly apologetic that I decided not to mention it. Instead, I asked, "Why?"

I expected him to say "Revenge," and I wouldn't have blamed him.

"I was pretty sure Miss Lindstrum would have us present our papers to the class. And I wanted Bruce Wyatt and Dennis Duffy to see that I have a life, a real life, and that I don't just sit home reading the encyclopedia. I wanted them to see me hanging around with someone like you." He dropped his head slightly. "Then maybe they'd think differently of me. I wanted them to respect me."

I wasn't sure what to say and it got very quiet for a minute or two. Malcolm was shuffling his feet around under the table; I looked down and noticed his sneakers. They were the wrong kind, as usual. They weren't the bulky basketball sneakers Bruce wore and was always bragging about. They weren't like the super-lightweight running shoes Dennis had, either. If Malcolm had wanted to earn some respect from the boys, all he would have had to do was ask Dr. Steve for a brand-new, expensive pair of gym shoes. But now, looking down at Malcolm's sneakers, it struck me that they looked perfectly comfortable. And somehow I knew that Malcolm would not be comfortable in any other sneakers, even the right ones.

I was about to respond, but before I could, Kate and Dr. Steve appeared. They weren't smiling. I felt myself move closer to Malcolm.

"Hannah," said Dr. Steve, attempting a grin, "why don't

you hurry and get dressed? We're going to head over to the—"

"What's wrong?"

"Well, Ian isn't responding to the medication as well as they'd hoped. His lungs are weaker than his doctors thought and, well"—the grin again—"let's just go over and see him, okay?"

I ran up the stairs to the guest room and put on the clothes I'd worn the day before. My hands were shaking as I tried to button my shirt. I gave up trying to tie my shoelaces after the fourth attempt.

I was out the front door in less than two minutes.

Back into the Mercedes. Back to the hospital.

The doctors were always explaining things.

Malcolm sat in a chair in the waiting room. I sat on my dad's lap; he was exhausted and frightened and that frightened me. He'd heard the explanation already. I was tired of Dr. Benedict explaining about distended muscles and the mucus that Ian would eventually be unable to expel. Ian's muscles were turning to fat at a much faster rate than they'd predicted. At this point, his case was worse than it was in most kids his age. The deterioration was accelerated, the doctor explained. (Accelerated, I thought, like being in the top reading group.) I wanted him to stop explaining—I wanted him to shut up and go help my brother.

"Is Ian going to die?" I asked. My voice sounded surprisingly calm. I was never calm when I spoke to a doctor; that's what made me realize that I wasn't asking the doctor. I was asking Malcolm.

Malcolm didn't give the doctor a chance to answer. "Yes," he said. "But not this time." He turned to Dr. Benedict, clicking his tongue. "Right?"

Dr. Benedict looked at my father; I guess you need permission from a parent to tell a kid her brother is going to die. Like going on a field trip, or missing gym. Why did these stupid thoughts keep coming into my mind—reading groups, field trips. I suppose I was just trying to get a handle on all this by translating it into things I understood.

Dad pulled me a little closer on his lap. Ian's doctor said, "Yes. I'm sorry, Hannah. This time, Ian will probably recover. But I can't promise you that next time . . ."

"Let's not worry about next time," said Malcolm, too much like a grownup. "Let's pull Ian through this and just hope that next time is very far away." He finished with a nod that made him seem even more adult. But I didn't want him to be an adult now. I wanted him to be a kid, with me. A smart, expert on muscular dystrophy kid, but a kid.

"So Ian is dying?" I said, hoping I'd gotten it wrong. Dad tried to say yes but the word never made it to his lips. "He's always been dying, is that it? He's been dying all along."

"Try not to think of it like that," the doctor said.

"How should I think of it?" I demanded. I know it was disrespectful to talk to him that way, but I couldn't help myself. The anger was taking over.

"Think of the good memories. Think of the times to come."

I sprung up from my father's lap and shouted, "Where'd you get that one, huh? Off a Hallmark card?"

Dad rubbed his eyes. "Hannah . . ."

I picked up an ashtray from the end table and threw it. I kicked a chair. I didn't recognize myself. No one tried to stop me. They let me scream and holler and trash the waiting room, because I guess they thought it would help.

But it didn't.

The only thing that helped was knowing that my friend

Malcolm Murgatroyd would be there when it was all over and we would remember Ian together, even when all that was left would be his room with the waist-high light switches and the deep wheel ruts in the carpet, his books, and those damn sneakers.

And the photos. The snapshots from the shore, from the barbecues, from Disney World. The ones Mom hadn't let me cut up for my autobiography. I'd wanted to chop up the pictures but I hadn't, and knowing that I still had them—would always have them—was a relief.

I stopped yelling and let the relief settle in. It was almost like happiness. *I didn't ruin the pictures.* It was something like courage, I think.

It may not have sounded like much, but when you find out your little brother is dying, you take what you can get.

twenty-two

IT WAS LATE THAT AFTERNOON. Outside, a snow flurry had begun. It made the sky look wide, deep, and at once full of darkness and light.

Malcolm and I were sitting on the foot of Ian's bed, playing a hushed game of Go Fish and waiting for him to wake up from his nap.

"Look at the sky," I whispered. "It's gloomy and bright at the same time."

"Like us," Malcolm whispered back.

I picked up a jack and slid it into my hand. Except for the sound of the cards and Ian's strained breathing, the room was quiet. Something had been bothering me and I wanted to get it off my chest. "What do you think will happen if you and I don't . . . you know . . . get married?"

He looked at me in disbelief. "What do you mean?"

"I mean, will our parents be mad? Will they go crazy? What'll happen?"

Malcolm put his cards down and stared at me for a long moment. "Hannah," he whispered, "it's a joke."

"What's a joke?"

"The whole wedding thing. You knew that, didn't you?"

I studied my cards. I didn't know that. All these years, all the talk about me and Malcolm growing up and getting married and Mom and Dad and Kate and Steve dancing at the wedding hadn't seemed like a joke to me.

"You thought they were serious," said Malcolm.

"They sounded serious," I whispered. "They sounded like they were counting on it." My throat was dry and my cheeks flushed. I felt stupid and unconnected—they all knew and I didn't. No wedding? For the moment, at least, I wanted to be able to see something definite in my future.

"Well," said Malcolm gently, "maybe they thought it was a good idea when we were babies. But as we got older and they saw how different we were, they must've figured out that it was an impossibility."

I couldn't tell if it hurt him to admit this. And who knew? If all Mom's late-bloomer stuff turned out to be true, maybe it wouldn't be so bad, at that. And even if he never bloomed into another Dr. Steve, even if he stayed a nerdy little bud forever, what would be so awful about that? Malcolm had a lot of other things going for him.

Before I could say this, though, Malcolm said, "You're just not my type."

My mouth dropped open. "What?"

"No offense, Hannah. I just think I'd be better off marrying someone else more like me, with similar interests."

This was incredible. Malcolm was as opposed to marrying me as I'd been to marrying him. And all this time I'd been assuming that he was hoping for it, planning on it, just like our parents—who, as it turned out, hadn't been planning on it at all.

I looked at Malcolm and he looked at me. Then he said, "Go fish."

Ian woke up about twenty minutes later. He could barely speak, but he gave us a grin and managed to say hello.

"Boy," I teased, holding his hand. "Some kids will do anything for a little attention."

His smile broadened and he fought to get the words out. "Are you guys . . . are you guys . . . friends now?" he asked.

"Yeah," I told him. "We're friends."

"Oh, we were always friends," said Malcolm. "We just didn't know it."

"Yeah," I said again, and I knew he was right.

The days that followed were filled with waiting. I was jumpy and sleepless, and mostly overwhelmed. Sometimes I felt helpless; other times, hopeful and sure. Sometimes Mom and I would sit in the hospital cafeteria and drink hot chocolate, or Dad and I would run out for burgers and hot dogs and bring them back to Malcolm and Dr. Steve and we'd picnic in the waiting room. The doctors would tell us that Ian was making great strides and we'd toast my brother's progress with our milk shakes and 7UPs.

At home, in the evenings, I'd go through old photographs and work on my autobiography. I'd already handed in a copy, the day Ian got sick. This was a new version. The true version. And in the afternoons, Malcolm would sit on Ian's hospital bed and check the spelling.

Every day, the hospital seemed farther away and the drive there seemed longer.

One morning, Mom and I sat at the kitchen table, waiting for Dad to come downstairs. Mom stirred her coffee absently, focusing on the sloping triangles of frost in the corners of the windowpanes.

"Hannah . . ." she said softly, placing her teaspoon in the saucer. "Hannah, I'm so sorry."

I was about to bite into an English muffin but her apology

froze me and the muffin hung there in front of my mouth. "For what?"

"For all of this, for everything you're going through."

"But it's not your fault!" I couldn't believe what I was hearing. "And besides, you and Daddy are going through it, too."

She nodded; her face looked strained, as if she were fighting something back. Then she said, "Yes, we're going through it, too. But Ian, he's . . . oh, my baby . . ." She broke off and pressed her fingers hard against her lips, as if trying to trap the words inside. I waited; she went on. "You can't imagine how it feels to watch your child . . . suffer." She was going to say "die"; she said "suffer," instead. I thought of Kate watching Malcolm suffer through all those years of being picked on.

I stood up and walked around the table to put my arms around her. "I'm okay, Mom."

"Yes!" she said quickly. "Yes, you are. You're okay. Thank goodness, you're okay."

It took a minute for this to sink in, but when I understood, it was like a stab in the heart. I was healthy, I didn't have MD. But Ian did, and Mom felt responsible. She thought it was her fault. I remembered what Dr. Benedict told us back at the beginning about muscular dystrophy being passed from a mother to her children. Mom was telling me she was sorry because she gave it to him.

I was going to remind her of all the other things she'd given him—the big, brown eyes with the long lashes, and his spunky sense of humor. And all the care: bathing him, helping him go to the bathroom, dressing him, just loving him. But somehow I knew it wouldn't help.

Then Dad appeared and said, "Ready, ladies?"

Mom stood quickly and gave me a brave, secretive smile. It said, Let's not get Daddy upset. That was fine. This was between my mother and her "female child," but I did not allow myself to think about that monster under the bed, or what it might mean someday, a long time from then.

I smiled, too. No, let's not get Daddy upset. Because it feels horrible to watch your parents suffer, too.

twenty-three

"HE SOUNDS FASCINATING!" said Dr. Emily Porter, leaning on her desk. "And very special."

I was sitting in her office in a big, fat chair with a swivel bottom. I swung to the right and studied the framed diplomas on her wall. "He is special," I said, swinging back to face her. "It helps to have him around."

"And it helps Ian, too, doesn't it?"

"Yes."

I liked Dr. Emily Porter very much. She was the family therapist Dr. Benedict recommended. He said it would be very important to, as he put it, "get in touch with our feelings," and that she would be able to help us to "put things into perspective." For the last forty minutes, we'd been putting Malcolm into perspective.

I thought for a long time before I said, "It's going to be difficult, holding on and letting go at the same time. To Ian, I mean." I leaned forward because my words came quickly, as quickly as my thoughts, and I was afraid I might miss them. "And the time will go fast and slow at the same time, too. And one day, just when we think we're going to be able to hold on for good, we'll have to let go. That's how it's going to happen, isn't it?"

"I think so," said Dr. Emily with a slight nod. "Yes."

"It reminds me of a song," I said suddenly. "Would you like to hear it? It's a song we used to sing when we were little. Malcolm helped me remember it."

Dr. Emily leaned back in her chair. "I'd love to hear it."

I sang it for her and she smiled. "It's a nice song, isn't it?"

"Yes, it is."

"It works good on nightmares," I told her, and was surprised to hear how young I sounded. "Even on the ones that come true."

Ian finally responded to the antibiotics and beat the pneumonia. This time.

"Let's not worry about next time," Malcolm had said at the hospital, and those became the words we lived by.

Ian came home a week later and started crashing into furniture again. It was the most wonderful sound we'd ever heard.

I'd missed almost two weeks of school and was almost glad to be going back. Evie met me in the girls' lav my first day.

"How's it going?" she asked.

"Good," I said, smiling. "How's it going here?"

"Okay. Everybody was worried. Even Sheila."

For a split second, I actually had to stop and think who Sheila was. Really. She was so insignificant that I'd practically forgotten her. "Oh. Hey, how were the autobiographies?" I asked.

Evie made a face. "Bored me to tears, most of them. Some were okay. Bruce's was mostly statistics—his batting averages from the last five years. His time in the hundred-yard dash." She paused to smear on some Mad About Melon, which didn't look so bad after all. "Did you know Alex Delaney has an older sister who's deaf?"

"No," I said. "I didn't know that." I never knew much about Alex Delaney.

"Well," said Evie, snapping the cap back on her lip gloss. "At least you got out of reading yours."

I gave her a tiny smile but said nothing. We left the girls' lav just as Malcolm, the hall monitor, was about to knock and tell us to get to class.

"Hi, Malcolm," I said.

"Howdy, Hannah."

Evie took a deep breath. "Hello, Malcolm." Then she smiled, as if she'd been expecting it to be painful but was surprised to find out that it wasn't.

"Pleasure to see you, Evie," said Malcolm. It wouldn't have been Malcolm if he'd just said hi. I laughed to myself.

The classroom became suddenly quiet when I walked in. From the corner, Bruce gave me a wave. I nodded hello and went directly to Miss Lindstrum's desk.

"How are you, dear?"

"Fine, thank you."

"And how's your brother?"

It was such an enormous question. I gave her a tiny answer: "Better."

I handed her the pile of assignments I'd done that week at home. Then I said, "Miss Lindstrum, if it's not too much trouble, I was wondering if you'd let me do something." I leaned down and made my request quietly.

She patted my arm when she said, "Of course."

Malcolm came in and removed his hall-monitor badge.

After attendance and lunch count, Miss Lindstrum cleared her throat and said, "People, Hannah is going to read her autobiography for us today. I expect you to give her your undivided attention."

No one groaned or rolled his eyes, which was the standard

reaction to someone presenting a paper to the class. I suppose they figured that this autobiography, given the events of the last two weeks, would contain some interesting plot twists.

I walked to the front of the room and opened the report cover. The paper made a crisp, clean sound—it was an honest sound, like the sound of truth.

"My name is Hannah Billings," I read. "I was born on February 3 and I am in sixth grade. I have one brother, Ian, who has muscular dystrophy."

I saw Malcolm out of the corner of my eyes and for a second I pictured him sitting on a desk tossing a football up and down. I read the part about how we found out Ian had MD, the parts about the hurricane, the training wheels, the nightmares, and each time I read Malcolm's name, I felt a small shadow of the happiness—the courage—I'd felt that day at the hospital.

When I got to the last page, I paused and looked up from the report; I knew the last line by heart. "My future plans include going to college, doing volunteer work for the Muscular Dystrophy Foundation, and someday, if I'm lucky, marrying someone like Malcolm Murgatroyd."

Which is exactly what I did.